# DEN OF THIEVES

## DESERT CURSED SERIES, BOOK 7

### SHANNON MAYER

HiJINKS

Mayer, Shannon
Den of Thieves, Desert Cursed Series Book 7

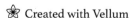 Created with Vellum

## ACKNOWLEDGMENTS

Thank you to the readers who loved Zam, Lila and Maks enough to want to see what comes next! I hope you enjoy their adventure and have as much fun reading it as I did writing it!

*Hope is a lover's staff; walk hence with that*
*And manage it against despairing thoughts.*
*Will Shakespeare*

A teeny tiny speck in the air a mile or so ahead of us was the only indication of Lila scoping out the land. While she was a dragon, and a monstrous foe when she wanted to be, more often than not, she stayed in her smaller form where she had a wingspan of two and a half, maybe three feet, at best. Weighing in at six pounds and able to get in and out of tight spots, she only pulled out the big guns—her *I'm so big I could carry a horse if I wanted to* size—when necessary.

I watched closely as she slowed over a spot in the desert I couldn't see, spiraling to the ground with a flash of blue scales, then as quickly as a bolt from a crossbow, shot into the air. Hovering there, she didn't move, didn't shift into her larger form. Nor did she fly back our way.

So not too scary but intriguing enough to stay where she was and watch . . . whatever it was she was observing.

"What's going on?" I muttered.

Balder jigged under me, snorting and then tossing his head, his lightly dappled gray coat damp with nervous sweat. I stroked a hand down his neck, picking up on his rising energy. Or maybe he was picking up on mine. While he might have looked like just a horse, he was in fact, a unicorn minus the horn.

No. Really, my horse was a freaking unicorn. I'd only recently discovered that, and I had to admit all the signs had been there for years. I'd just ignored them. Speed like no other, quicker recovery time, intelligence that was on par with any person I knew. That and he had his own brand of magic, the ability to gift others with skillsets they otherwise wouldn't have.

Basically, he was a gem in all the ways possible.

I patted his neck again and narrowed my eyes as Lila continued to circle around whatever it was she'd come across.

"What do you think?" Maks's rumble soothed any worries that bubbled under my skin, and my heart rate immediately eased. I glanced at him.

Messy blond hair that brushed the back of his neck, blue eyes, solid body, soft lips, and a strong jaw. More than that, good heart, gentle hands, and so damn smart, it made me want to throw my clothes at him.

His hands rested lightly on his horse's neck, scratching Batman gently as he kept his eyes on Lila ahead of us.

Batman—yes, I know it's a strange name, some would even say dumb for a horse, but I didn't name him and he came when called, so there you have it—stretched his neck and nipped at Balder who just ignored him.

"We knew the quiet wouldn't last. I thought we'd have till we reached the Blackened Market." I thought about the last two weeks, about the slow ride south as we headed to the last known location of the dragon eggs we were tracking. About the lazy mornings, and the lovemaking when Lila was off hunting, the laughter as the fire crackled late into the night and the joy in being free of fear for a little bit.

Then again, there were things that made me jumpy, like the croak of a frog, or the rumble of distant thunder. Things that made me tense when they came upon us, because in the past, those things had been deadly. I shook my head, clearing it of the thoughts that rolled through me.

"Let's check it out. She's not too worried by the looks of it." I gave Balder a cue to step out, and he went right into a quick trot. "Eager much?" I leaned back and gave him a scratch on the hip. Feisty and always ready to run at top speed, he was ready to gallop to Lila if I so much as leaned forward.

I sat back farther, slowing him just a bit. There was no rush. If this was the end of our quiet, I wanted to enjoy the moment. Such as it was.

As we drew closer to Lila, I could make out the object on the ground. Or more accurately, the creature.

Hunched over on itself, I could make out spotted hide, a short tail, limbs that were powerful but squat, and I found myself reaching for a weapon I no longer had to deal with a creature that every lion hated.

Hyenas.

Or, in this case, one hyena. But why had Lila flown away like she had, straight up as if she were afraid? A single hyena was no match for Lila.

Before I could call out to my winged sister-friend, she swept our way on a down draft, fanned her wings and landed on the pommel of my saddle, gripping it with glittering sharp claws, balancing easily.

"Her wit's as thick as a Tewkesbury mustard.

And she's freaky as shit," she said, then patiently waited with her eyes bright. "Zam?"

I shook my head. "Let Maks try first. It's not fair to show him up every time."

Lila snickered and stretched her neck and head toward Maks.

Maks tapped a hand on his thigh, drumming his fingers. "I should know that one. It sounds familiar. Have you used it before?"

I gave him another ten seconds before I answered. It was our game. Drop an insult from Shakespeare and have one of the others guess the literary source. Lila and I were rarely stumped. Maks, on the other hand, was still trying to catch us. "*Henry IV*. Lila, do you mean to say the hyena *talked* to you?"

You see, there were shifter hyenas in the desert, but they tended to be larger than the average hyena, at least triple the size and weight. This hyena we were closing in on was smaller than the average hyena, not larger.

"I mean, yes, sort of. But that isn't what's freaky. I'll let you decide that for yourself." Lila crawled onto my shoulder and wrapped her tail around my neck for balance. "I mean . . . really freaky."

Great. Just what we were not looking for. A freaky assed hyena that talked.

We closed the distance to twenty feet and

then I pulled up short. The last thing I wanted was one of the horses getting bit. I slid off Balder's back and reached for a couple of my smaller knives I kept strapped to my body. One on my left thigh and one pressed against my lower back in a sheath that Maks had made for me on this trip.

"Hyena, do you speak?" I approached the creature slowly, knees bent, muscles tensed and ready to send me in any direction. I stopped ten feet away.

The hyena shuddered and rolled to face me, showing off her belly in a move that was as submissive as could be. "Don't kill me," she said and then giggled hard and fast, maniacal. "Killing me would be bad for you, bad for your mate, bad for your sister."

Her coat flickered as though she had something crawling around inside of her, the flesh bulging and then receding over and over again, all over her.

"Freaky ass shit indeed." I didn't take a step closer. "Hyena, what ails you?"

Her whole body shivered. "The beast is taking its dues, and all those who walk on four legs will be called home."

"Tewkesbury mustard," Lila muttered in my ear. "Nutty."

"Is it nutty?" I'd never had mustard by that name; I had no idea.

Lila leaned forward. "Hyena, do you mean us harm?"

The hyena kept shivering. "No, no, I am . . . a warning to all who pass through these lands into the east. Taken from you, the powers will be humbled to the ground, spells are cast, a new power rises, there is no escaping the touch of the beast. He comes for the west."

I found myself crouching so her eyes were level with mine. Sharp intelligence stared back at me, eyes far too human for any creature who was animal alone. "Are you a shaman?"

"Was, I was. I ran, and ran, but the power caught me and trapped me as this, but not before it shoved me full of death. I am dying. I am, and so I warn you. Bright ones, go wary into the desert of the east, go wary or don't go at all."

Another shiver and her fur bulged, cracks appearing here and there. "Do you wish me to end it?"

She shook her head. "You killed the son of the Emperor, the magician. I saw it in my dreams. I saw you right the balance of the western desert. But there is always a power waiting to take the reins. That power rises now. Bright ones, this power is dark, far darker than the magician's magic. His was made of manipulation, of turning hearts against hearts, of trickery."

She drew a shuddering breath. "This one . . . his is naught but death. And you . . . if you walk into the east, you will find more than you bargain for. Beware, the north will test you."

I glanced at Maks who'd crept closer. We both were eye level with the hyena who writhed at our feet, whimpering between her words. I opened my mouth to ask her a question, but she cut me off with a yipping cry.

"My death will come, but I give you what words I can. He gathers an army. He will take the east and the west if he is not stopped." Pain-filled eyes locked on mine. "Do you understand, Zamira, guardian of the desert? Do you understand, Lila, guardian of the skies? Do you understand, Maks, guardian of the bright ones?"

I nodded. Lila nodded. Maks nodded.

A sigh slid from her. "Then I have warned you. Will you go on?"

I didn't need to look at my friends to know that answer. "This beast, he will come for the west? That's what you're saying?"

"Yes," she whispered and shuddered again. "I escaped him. I knew I'd find you here before the Blackened Market. I saw it in my dreams. You have a chance now. Seek out an army of your own, and you will face him on the fields of poppies. The flowers will hide the blood that rains upon the ground." Her skin popped in several places and a sigh slid out of her as if air from a balloon was being released.

As we watched, her skin and bones seemed to melt, sinking into the dry desert ground, the sand soaking in everything she was until there was nothing, not even a mark to claim her passing.

I stared at that spot and wrinkled my nose as I whispered a quiet prayer for her passing. "Time's really up for us then."

Lila snorted and tightened her hold on my shoulder. "Well, if that isn't a start to a shitty day, I'm not sure what is."

## 2

———

Maks put his hand on my elbow as we turned back toward the horses after watching the messenger dissolve into the desert ground. "I know you, Zam." I kicked my feet through the sand not yet hot from the morning sun.

"Uh-huh, I know you too," I winked up to him, "in the most biblical of senses."

His lips quirked and the smile that wasn't truly on his mouth was there in his eyes. "I'm talking about knowing how you are, and how you think. I don't expect you to not want to deal with this beast the hyena was talking about. But we are on the hunt for dragon eggs that have been stolen—we gave our word to find them."

I slid my hand over his and locked fingers with

him, just long enough to give him a squeeze. "I know. But this is a warning. Whatever is going on in the east, blazing in blind is stupid. I'll take a heads-up for a new nasty any day."

He didn't let me go, but instead tugged me closer so our lips brushed against one another. Lila stuck her face between us, claw tips digging into each of our cheeks as she pushed us apart. "None of that when I'm on your shoulders. Sucking face all the time like a couple of horny teenagers. Act your ages, will you?"

I threw my head back and laughed. "I wasn't going to kiss him, Lila."

"Speak for yourself," Maks muttered. "I was totally going to suck face with you."

Lila grumbled and waved a tiny fist at him as though she were an old man on his front porch, yelling at kids as they disrupted his peace. Which only made me laugh all the more.

"Look," I finally said as I pulled myself onto Balder's back, my laughter slowing. "A warning is good. I don't see us deliberately looking for this beast. We are looking for the missing dragon eggs, that's our priority. I completely agree with you."

I felt their eyes heavily on me. I turned and Lila and Maks had the same look on their faces, despite being very different species.

Disbelief was etched plainly there. "You basically got called out by a shaman hyena to protect the desert. And you're not going to listen?" Lila asked.

I threw my hands in the air. "You both just said you didn't want me looking for this beast. I said I wouldn't. Now you want me to?"

"No," Lila said. "But what if the eggs are tied to him? Would that be so *unfathomable*?"

"Good word," Maks said. Lila launched off my shoulder, flew to his, and then gave him a tiny high five.

I stared over the endless brown ground, thinking, trying to put together what lay ahead of us, but I was no seer of the future. What I could see was the edge of the Blackened Market. Burned down, destroyed, but it was where the trail of the dragons' eggs picked up. A beast from the east, huh? Maybe it was just a warning because whoever had the eggs saw us coming and thought to scare us off. Maybe it was a hyena pulling one last joke, which was not so out of the ordinary for the creatures.

But the image of the hyena's skin pulsing and popping as though something else lived inside her was rather fresh in my mind and there was no joke about how she'd died. Which meant I wasn't about to discount her final words.

"Let's see what the market has to offer first," I said, "then we go from there."

Lila and Maks gave each other a look and I stuck my tongue out at them. Childish, but it broke the knot of tension that had been tangling inside my guts. Those who could see some bits and pieces of the future, like shamans, really shouldn't be ignored. Not that they were always right, but by the same token, their words could be used to avoid shitty endings. I didn't want a shitty ending for any of us after all we'd been through.

The two horses picked up on the swirling energy and broke into a quick trot covering the ground at a steady pace. Balder stretched his nose out enough to be in front. Batman could have tried to beat him, but he was not the boss of the two of them and didn't like being in the lead. Try telling Balder that, though.

He stretched farther, putting distance between us and Maks and Batman. I didn't try to hold him back because I was eager to see what the Blackened Market—or what was left of it—held for us in terms of clues.

Lila had grown up in the Dragon's Ground, and for years, a huge portion of the unhatched eggs had been stolen. Seeing as dragons were not the most prolific of breeders, those losses were a blow not only to the mothers, but to the entire population as well.

Maks and I had promised the female dragons we'd find their babies and bring them back. A promise I didn't regret, but wondered just how the hell I was going to manage to keep it when we had so little information to go on. Which brought us here to the Blackened Market. Truly blackened now, razed by fire in a fight that we may or may not have started. I narrowed my eyes, looking over the scene. The charred and broken timbers of the buildings, the sand crystalized in places from the heat.

The marks of blades that had cut deep into the wood.

The ground where it had been flattened by something, or many somethings.

"This happened after we left." I reached out to touch a charred piece of wood, feeling the chunk where a blade had bit fully into it.

Balder slowed and I hopped off before he had completely come to a standstill. Lila was there in a flash of blue and silvery scales, doing her trademark loops through the air. A sure sign of her own tension.

The ground had the strangest tracks on it, or maybe they weren't tracks at all. I bent low over one close to the edge of the remnants of a building.

It was a wide foot, super flat, and two-toed. I spread my fingers over it and wasn't able to span the width of the foot. Whatever it was attached to was a big boy.

But it was no dragon.

"This wasn't Corvalis, was it?" I said as I walked onto what had been the main thoroughfare of the market. Corvalis was Lila's father, the nut-job, power-hungry ex-leader of the dragons. Lila had killed him and proven her worth as his successor. We'd assumed that he'd been the one to set fire to the market after we'd left it at a dead gallop.

Lila swept over a few of the charred buildings, inspecting what was left of the destruction. "No, this was no dragon. Though I think it was done to make it look that way to anyone who doesn't know much. Hence the burning of the buildings to a crisp."

I made my way east on the strip, poking the toe of my boot into a few bits and pieces, pausing at the place that had been the weapons stall. A half-dozen timbers were down, and the leftover mud that had held the buildings together was crumbled everywhere.

My hand went over my shoulder to where the handle of my flail had been. A flail that had saved my life more than once, but that I'd had to give up to save the world and all that jazz. That being said,

I needed a new weapon. One that wouldn't break under the first blow. I had a couple of knives, but they would only do so much. I wiggled my nose, drawing in a deep breath to see if I could pick up the smell of any iron under the burned-out rubble.

Nothing.

I curled my nose up and crouched by the debris, breathing deep. Still nothing. Not even a hint of something. Maks crouched beside me. "Anything useable?"

Without a doubt, he knew what I was looking for. More likely he'd seen me reach for the weapon that was no longer on my back. I pushed a chunk of rubble out of the way. "Nope."

"We'll find you something. Besides, you can shift to your jungle cat form, and you and Balder have all this magic mojo going on. Lila can be two sizes of dragon, and I still have my Jinn abilities. We'll be okay without another weapon for a bit." He gave me a wink.

Lila buzzed down over our heads, a bottle in her claws. "And țuică! I found a bottle!"

Before she could fly away, I leapt up and grabbed the bottle of liquor made from plums that we all liked a little too much, and promptly threw it onto the ground. "Are you crazy?"

Spluttering and pointing, her tail flipping in serious agitation, she sliced through the air with a sharp whistle. "Me? You're the one who broke that bottle of amazing-ness!" She tucked her wings and flew for the ground, heading straight for the rapidly dissipating liquid. I kicked sand over the wet spot, just in case she decided she was desperate enough to try lapping it up.

By the violet-eyed glare she gave me, that was exactly what she was thinking of doing.

"You remember the last time you drank it? It knocked you out for three days and stole your ability to shift sizes." I pointed at her. "People know you're a closet kleptomaniac when it comes to this plum juice. So enough. Find something new to drink."

Grumbling, she turned her back on me and strode down the street in a huff, kicking dirt behind her, each step creating a tiny dust cloud. A smile crept over my face as I watched her go. Every once in a while she punctuated her grumbles with a claw, or a flick of her tail. Maybe if she'd been in her larger form, her movements would have been intimidating instead of funny.

Maks looped an arm around my waist. "What do you want to bet she finds a bottle of something else before sundown?"

I smiled up at him. "Counting on it. She has a nose for booze; it's crazy."

His eyes met mine, and he bent his head,

kissing me. Soft and sweet with a layer of heat underneath that made every bone in my body turn to jelly. I held onto him to keep my legs under me. I didn't take this for granted—him, this love, the life we had—even if it was wandering a desert and looking for dragon eggs.

The last few weeks had been as close to perfect as I could have hoped. He pulled back a bit, our foreheads touching as we both fought to keep our breath. "Zam."

"Yes?"

"Just wanted to say your name." Maks closed the distance to kiss me again. "To taste it in my mouth."

Damn it, he said all the right things. I slid my arms around his neck. My lips had barely touched his when a small body slammed into us, grabbing at our shoulders, blue and silver scales all I could see for a split second.

"Lila, what the hell?" I grabbed her, irritation fleeing as her panic slid through me, the trembling in her body running the length of her. "Lila, what's wrong?"

"I swear I didn't drink any of the țuică! But I can't shift," she whispered. "I'm stuck again."

## 3

The remainder of the Blackened Market let my words echo out across the air. Or maybe I was yelling more than I wanted. "You drank the țuică, didn't you?" I tried to keep my voice even, honest. I'd literally just broken the bottle of țuică, and Lila had gone and found another and drank it already? Damn it. I mean, they couldn't all be poisoned with magical spells, but then, what did I know?

"No, no, I didn't! I swear I didn't!" She whipped around our heads, frantic. "I . . . I walked to the end of the market strip and when I got to the end, I thought I'd shift and come back and . . . take you for a flight."

I doubted that. More likely she'd have tried to scare us for breaking her țuică, but whatever. That wasn't the point. "Okay, show us where you were. Maybe there is something you tripped, like a spell? Maybe it's something Maks can fix."

Balder and Batman followed the three of us down the length of the Blackened Market strip. Lila zipped in loops in front of us. "I was just walking down here, talking to myself and thinking maybe I could scare you two," I glanced at Maks and he gave a subtle nod, "and I was feeling kind of excited, right, like right before a hunt. And then I got to the end of the strip and turned around and tried to shift and there was nothing." She shot to my shoulder, knocking me back a half-step. Her tiny claws dug into me as she gripped harder than normal.

"Easy, Lila. We will figure this out." I slowed as we approached the end of the market strip.

Maks lifted one hand, palm down, and did a slow circle. I scanned the area with my eyes, waiting on him to find something first. We both had Jinn magic, but he was far more trained in the use of it. I'd only just discovered the magic running through my veins, and mine was wilder, unpredictable and powerful, as per being a female Jinn. Training didn't seem to want to work with me when it came to my magic; it mostly seemed to run on need for me.

"I'm not picking anything up." His blue eyes

narrowed as he looked over the rubble, clenching his hand into a fist. "You?"

"I'm terrible at this," I said.

"No time like the present to try," he pointed out. "Use both hands, slow your breathing, let the magic come to the surface instead of trying to force it."

With a grimace, I held both hands out, palms facing the road.

I did as he said, slowing my breathing, and tried to let the magic rise on its own. Almost leisurely, it flowed to my fingertips, like a snobby horse, feigning interest to see if I had anything worth working for.

Fingertips tingling, heat exploded down my arms. From leisurely to violent intensity, the Jinn magic was suddenly fire in my blood, coursing through me, waiting in my hands like an eager horse at the start of race. Testing me. So much for wondering if I had anything worth working for.

I curled my fingers ever so slightly as if I were holding reins. "Easy," I whispered.

The magic settled a little, apparently satisfied.

With my eyes still closed, I swept my hands out, waiting for something to set off the magic.

There was nothing specific, but a tug on my feet, like a rope around my ankles urging me to move, calling me. I stepped forward, following it.

Another tug, and another, like a gentle whisper that was just outside of reach.

"You feel that?" I asked. "Lila, did you feel anything before you realized you couldn't shift?"

She shook her head fiercely. "No, I was busy talking to myself. I was working on my next Shakespeare quote that I was going to use when I scared you."

My lips curled upward. Of course, she was.

The tug forward was gentle, soft, welcoming and so subtle that if I hadn't been looking for it, I might not have noticed it. I opened my eyes and watched the ground as I walked, looking for a symbol, something that would indicate a spell. "Maks?"

"Yes, I feel it now too. It's very . . . tender is the only word I have for it."

We reached the end of the market strip and I turned to face the way we'd come. Balder was right behind me, and I'd barely noticed him there, so focused on the magic that I was picking up on. He bumped me with his nose and gave a soft whinny. I flicked my fingers to disperse the magic, then ran a hand down the side of his face. "No idea what this is, buddy, no idea at all."

He bumped me harder and I looked at him, the way his eyes had rolled to show me white all around the edges. My stomach clenched with a pulse of fear. Another sharp whinny and he pawed at the ground. More than a horse, though I forgot because he had been like this with me for as long as I'd had him. No horn; it had been taken off to keep him safe from those who hunted his herds to near extinction, but who and what he was, was still his own kind of magic. From time to time, I picked up images from him in a sort of telepathy, and he'd more than once saved our hides.

"What?" I kept my hands on his neck, feeling him tremble. "Lila, go high, see if something is coming."

"On it." She launched off my shoulder and I held onto Balder. "My friend, what is it?"

I waited for something from him, a direction, or a picture in my mind.

Nothing.

A chill slid through me.

Balder banged both front hooves into the ground as if stomping a desert snake. I backed up a step and he shook his head, his frustration obvious.

I looked at Maks who shrugged, then looked to where Lila flew. "Anything?"

"Nothing for as far as I can see," she shouted as she spiraled down to us. "What could have taken away my ability to shift?"

Balder stomped the ground in answer to her

question and I looked at the earth below us. There was nothing different about it, no marks or lines, no major boom of power when we'd stepped onto this path.

"We've triggered something. Lila can't shift, Balder can't communicate with me . . ." I held my hand out and let my breathing slow again, welcoming up the Jinn magic. Any of the magic.

Bupkes, as my dad would have said. Nada. Nothing. Zilch. But even then, I wasn't terribly worried, because I'd been without magic most of my life, and for all I knew, it was a hiccup in my giddy-up.

I was trying not to freak out, though, because something that could just snatch all four sets of very different magic without us even realizing was . . . well, that was bad. "Maks, can you reach your magic now?"

I made myself watch as he flexed his hands, as the veins popped up in his forearms and his eyebrows dropped low over his sky-blue eyes.

"Shit," Maks whispered and blew out a heavy breath as if he'd been running hard.

"Nothing?" I asked, already knowing the answer but hoping to hell I was wrong.

"It's gone, my magic is completely gone. This isn't possible."

"Back up, down the street. Now!" I pushed

them ahead of me, moving them as quickly as I could.

Standing where we'd started at the western end of the market strip. Maks tried for his magic again with no result. Lila tried to shift. Balder tried to talk to me. And I couldn't touch any of the magic that I'd so recently found inside me.

Every last ability we had was gone.

"You should try shifting," Lila said. "What if you can't even do that?"

She was right.

I blew out a breath that flapped my lips. "Yeah, that would be the shits."

For me, shifting was like stepping through a doorway. On one side I was a human, and on the other, I was a six-pound house cat.

I shifted, blinked and found myself looking up at them from my house cat form. That was good. I, at least, had that ability. I tried for my other shape, the black jungle cat.

I didn't really expect it to manifest since shifting into the large feline form was newer even than the magic I had. But it came to me quickly, and I found myself on a set of much bigger paws.

"That's good," Lila said, hopping across to land on my back between my shoulder blades. "At least I can get a free ride if I need a break."

"You are always getting free rides," Maks said.

They bickered a moment, and I knew it was just how they were dealing with an unprecedented moment. It was a way to blow off the steam of anxiety jumping through all three of us.

I found myself staring out at the far end of the market, at the seemingly innocent place we'd stood, their voices flowing over me. Obviously, there was something terrible and powerful in the market itself, and hidden very well. Did it have anything to do with the Blackened Market being razed? Or was it someone, or something, else working here?

As I watched, four pale orbs shot up out of the ground, so fast and so faint that if I hadn't been watching, I'm not sure I would have seen them. And then they were gone, flying to the east. I blinked a few times.

"Did you see that?" I asked.

"What?" Lila tucked her head, bumping it against my cheek. "What do you see?"

I shook my head and shifted back to two legs, Lila clinging to me the entire time which told me just how upset she was. "It's gone now." I quickly described the orbs to her and Maks.

"I've no idea what they could be," Maks said. "Nothing that I know of fits that description."

"Hey, why don't you ask the old boys?" Lila said.

One of the other things that had saved our bacon was the fact that while the old Jinn masters had left off possessing Maks, much of their knowledge had stayed in his head. While it wasn't always at the front of his mind, he could access what they knew, and that knowledge was a gold mine. Kind of like his own personal library, though there did seem to be a few holes here and there.

Knowing our luck, this would be one of those holes.

Lila and I watched as Maks closed his eyes, and his breathing slowed.

He was quiet for a good minute before a low groan escaped him. "They have nothing on this sort of an event. It's like everything we've gained, everything we've fought for, was just snatched away. But by whom?"

Lila growled. "Yeah, I'd like to know who is doing this? If Merlin wasn't dead, I'd say it was him. Or the Emperor."

She wasn't wrong. Except Merlin was dead, and the Emperor, my grandfather, without any power so much as in his pinky finger left to him after I'd finished with him.

"This is a fucking mess," I muttered. No weapon, no direction for the dragon eggs, and now no magic or abilities we'd worked so hard to gain. I frowned. "The hyena, she said something like the power would be stripped? Shit, she was literally telling us to watch ourselves and we still walked right into it!"

"I feel like saying all the things we had in our arsenal out loud cursed us to lose them." Maks stared up at the bright blue sky as if the answer would be there.

I wasn't sure that was the case at all. But as that place between my shoulders began to itch, I had no doubt someone was watching us. Waiting to see if we'd run away or keep moving forward on our path.

"The hyena warned us. Warned us and we came here anyway." I grabbed Balder's reins and mounted. "We need to continue on. The dragon eggs and hatchlings aren't going to save themselves."

"We have no magic! I'm a shrimp again!" Lila yelped, hopping to stand on Balder's neck so she could glare at me, her big eyes watering with tears.

"How is that different from when we went to the Witch's Reign? We did that as little shits, with no magic, and we beat her. Maks wasn't using his Jinn magic then for fear it would bring his father down on us. And we survived. We survived the Dragon's Ground the same way. So we go on, we find the eggs, and figure out along the way who the hell stole our abilities. And we get them back. That's the plan."

Maks pulled himself up onto Batman. "I agree. We have no choice but to go forward now. Anything strong enough to take our magic with such subtlety won't be satisfied with that. Now with the Emperor and Merlin gone, there is a wide open desert for any other power that might come along. What if . . . what if whoever this is knows about the jewels? Sure, we destroyed them, but they might not know that."

My stomach clenched. Yeah, that would be bad. No magic, moving forward, and headed to the east where some unnamed beast awaited us.

Awesome, just fucking awesome. But maybe I grinned a little. Because I was, if nothing else, comfortable in the position of underdog—under-cat. Better to be treated as if we weren't capable and then come out on top. Better to be underesti-mated yet again. And hope it was enough to slink by the radars out there.

We rode east, leaving the Blackened Market behind, but not without looking back several times. Those orbs I'd seen, they'd been faint, barely visible, yet I was sure they'd been there. Were they what had taken our powers? Or were they what I'd felt watching us?

Maybe both.

I shook my head and urged Balder into a trot. This part of the desert was softer with loose sand and more than a trot would put more strain on the horses' legs than I wanted to right then, no matter that they were fit and used to different surfaces.

The last thing we needed was an injury when we had no way of healing it.

I shut down that thought as soon as it came up, part of me horrified that by thinking it, I would make it happen. Just like Maks had said talking about our abilities had jinxed us.

I wanted to ask Maks what his Jinn knowledge knew about the eastern side of the realm. Then again, he might actually know all on his own. He'd been raised by the Jinn and they were all about taking over territories and controlling other creatures. But again, I hesitated.

I couldn't even say why, and I didn't like it. I forced myself to speak.

"Maks?"

He turned his head and lifted his brows. "Yes?"

"Do you know much about this area we are going into?"

"You mean as we head toward the far eastern wall?" He sat deep in his saddle, his back slumping a little. "Probably not enough to help us."

I waited, knowing him well enough to see he

was gathering his thoughts. Lila, on the other hand, was not so patient.

"Come on, Toad! Spit it out!" She leapt between the two horses, landing on the pommel of Batman's saddle so she could reach out and grab Maks's shirt. "We haven't got all day."

"That's not true," Maks said with a grin. "We actually do have all damn day."

"You know what I mean!" She snapped her claws up at him as if that would hurry him up.

He sighed. "What little I know could fill not even a single page of paper. Marsum, when he was looking at territories to conquer, never looked at the east. I asked him once why. His answer was that some pots were better left unstirred. And the memories of the others are similar. Almost as if . . ."

My eyes widened, as did Lila's. "Marsum was afraid of what was in the east?"

Maks rolled his shoulders as if that thought made him as uncomfortable as it did me. "He never came right out and said it, but yeah, I think that was the case. Or he knew he was outmatched maybe. Maybe that was why Davin was trying to gather more power? There are mountains between us and the far eastern realm. Wide ranges that are extremely dangerous, full of wild creatures looking to hunt and kill. Not like the desert you cross to get to the base of the mountains."

He let out a deep breath and ran a hand through his hair.

I considered for a moment, gathering my thoughts. "You think that memories of the other Jinn masters could have been tampered with to keep the knowledge about the east from getting out?"

"I think the only other person who might be able to tell you anything is your grandfather," Maks said. "You think you could walk in the dreamscape to find him?"

I grimaced. "The dreamscape broke apart when everything went down."

And that left us with nothing to go on, our abilities stripped, and an unknown realm to face.

If only we'd truly understood then what we were up against, we might not have been so fucking flippant.

## 4

As we trekked through the desert beyond the Blackened Market, Lila flopped to the side of Batman's neck, hanging from his mane with one set of toe claws, her wings limp, her other arm flung over her eyes. A case of the dramatics that was good even for her. "Like a dull actor now, I have forgot my part, and I am out, even to a full disgrace."

"I know that one," Maks said, grinning wide. "*Coriolanus*. I think even I can say that it was scene five. And really, rather fitting with the poor acting there."

She rolled up to her feet and flew to me, blowing him a wet raspberry as she went by. "Fine. Mock my pain, Toad."

I caught her with one hand and tucked her in

close. While she was making fun by being ridiculous, she was also shaking hard. Because once more, we were at the mercy of the world with no big guns to back us up. And she more than any of us would feel that pinch.

"It will be okay, Lila," I said softly, squeezing her to me. "We'll figure this out. I promise."

Her big violet eyes stared up at me. "I don't want to figure it out. I want for life to not be so damn hard. I want us to have a break for once."

"That's the problem, nobody gets an easy life," I said. "And honestly, those few who do, how often are they the ones that cause more problems? Self-serving assholes. We at least solve problems."

She curled up in front of me and closed her eyes. "I hate problems. I want to kill them and bury them in a stinking bog. And then go drink a bottle of țuică until I can't see straight."

I didn't blame her. Part of me wanted to curl up and ignore the world, too, especially after all we'd been through.

"It will be okay. We aren't dead, and we are still together, so it will work out in the end." I held her a little tighter, knowing the words weren't just for her. They were for me too. I had to believe we would face this new challenge together.

Sweat dribbled down my arms and spine, and Balder and Batman glistened with moisture as the sun beat down on us. Moving during the day was not ideal, but until we found a place to rest, this was the plan.

I drank from the waterskin regularly, offering it to Balder and Lila too. Maks did the same for him and Batman. We had to keep moving until there was somewhere to stop; no point in stopping out in the middle of the heat.

At the apex of the day, when the heat was the worst, I thought my eyes might be fooling me. The shade of a small cluster of rocks beckoned in the distance. I pointed at them. "Maks, there, that would work, I think."

"Yeah, that should give us enough cover. Looks like we might not be the only travelers out here, though." He pointed to the left of the rocks at the subtlest of movement from a cluster of smaller bodies.

Good people or bad, good monster or bad. Which would it be today? With how the day started . . . "I'm putting money on two assholes, a whiny sidekick, and too much loot to carry from the other people they robbed."

Maks looked across at me, his eyes sparkling as he deadpanned. "That sounds like us. Minus the loot, of course."

I couldn't help it, I laughed way harder than I should have—yeah, I knew I could be an asshole.

Lila, on the other hand, shot across to him. Apparently, she'd not been sleeping all that deeply.

"I am not whiny! I'm pissed off!" She took a swing at him that he barely dodged.

Maks caught her and pulled her into a hug. "I *know* you're not whiny. I'm not happy either, but until we can get some information, what are we to do? Wallow? No, that's not our style, Lila. I was teasing. I was just teasing."

She relaxed in his arms and then patted his cheek with one claw. "You're lucky I love you, Maks, or I'd claw your eyes out and pop them like grapes."

He kissed her on the nose. "I know I am."

Lila flipped herself out of his arms and swooped down low between the horses, her wings stretched wide. "I'll go check it out. Might as well make my whiny ass useful for something."

I watched her go and then looked across at Maks. He winked at me. "I figured she'd take offense."

"Oh, I knew what you were up to." I sobered quickly. "But I'm worried, Maks. I mean. I can live without my magic. I have for most of my life. But who the hell could snatch it like that without us even feeling it?" We hadn't talked much about it, the three of us lost in our own thoughts.

He nodded. "That's my concern too. That and

the fact that the Jinn masters' knowledge on that area is like a giant blank, which is more than worrisome. If you had the world divided into pages, each page giving you information on different parts of the world, the page for the east . . . that page has nothing on it. They even knew some stuff about the new world before the walls went up. But the east? Nothing."

I didn't like the shiver that cut through me. "That cannot be good. This beast from the east must be some seriously bad mojo."

"Agreed. I can't help feeling like . . . like this might be a game. And that was the first move. But to draw us in, or scare us away? Neither is good, and until we know, we are playing blind."

I nodded, and Balder matched me, bobbing his head up and down rapidly. Watching Lila fly ahead, I kept my eyes on the small figures around the rocks. They seemed to be . . . "Are they dancing?"

"Looks like it to me," Maks said. "But is it happy dancing, or the kind of dancing when you stub a toe?"

Or the kind of dancing some species did before they attacked?

That was the question, wasn't it? I asked Balder to pick up speed. A faster trot really was all I wanted, but he tried to bolt into a gallop. I slowed him down. "Yeah, how about we don't break our legs today in the loose sand and burn ourselves out of the last of our reserves?"

He blew out a snort and settled into a ground-covering trot, extending his legs out as far as he could without breaking into a gallop. Fair enough.

The air felt good on my face, drying some of the sweat, so I let him have a little more leeway in the speed department.

Batman slowed as we scooted forward. I looked over my shoulder and cursed. Batman had been given more speed and more stamina as a gift from Balder during our travels, because Balder was a horse that wasn't truly a horse, and no other true equine could ever keep up to him without help.

That gift to Batman was apparently gone too. "Damn it," I muttered. "Whoever took all our goodies is going to get nut sacked. Hard. At least three times."

A cry from Lila whipped me around as she plummeted to the ground, lines of black wrapped around her. Anger snapped up through me. Who the fuck did these creatures think they were messing with?

"Okay, now you can run." I gave a low hiss to Balder and he leapt forward, his legs eating up the distance between us and the dancing-whatever-they-were and a falling-from-the-sky Lila.

Balder stretched out and I leaned over his neck. As we drew close enough that I could see the creatures, my brain struggled to make sense of what they were.

Three feet tall at best, they were dressed in bright red robes, had hair the color of corn silk, and huge blue eyes that dominated their faces. They looked almost like cherubs. Minus the wings.

"Hey!" I hollered as I got close enough to see that they had netted Lila but hadn't hurt her. "What the fuck do you think you're doing?"

The group of them—thirteen on a quick count of their bright shining gold heads—turned to me as a unit. And bowed.

"We have waited. Our mistress told us to wait here. And you have come." They whispered together, but not together. Like they were a little off so the words reverberated around us like a weird echo that made my skin crawl and called up the urge to reach for a weapon I no longer had.

"Waited for what?"

Hell, I knew the answer, or I thought I did.

They pointed not at me, but at Lila. "We have waited for the little queen to arrive. She said she would come, and she was the marker of what we should wait for."

I hopped off Balder and stalked through the little weirdos, pushing them away from Lila. None of them had weapons that I could see, and they didn't push back. She glared up at them even though they seemed genuine about honoring her.

With a quick slash from one of my hunting knives, I cut the ropes loose over her and she popped up, hissing and spitting, acid flicking from her mouth.

The red-robed creatures went to their knees, bowed forward and put their heads to the ground in a perfect circle around her.

"I'm no one's queen," she said. "I'm just me."

The thing was, she had killed her father, Corvalis, who'd been a tyrant and the leader of the dragons. So, technically, they weren't wrong. She was the heir apparent, even if she had left Dragon's Ground without taking the throne.

"You are the daughter of the old ruler, which makes you queen, and now you are here. You brought with you companions to serve you?" The one who'd spoken first before lifted his head. Or I assumed it was the same one, they all looked alike.

"Why did you net her if you want to bow to her?" Maks asked as he drew up with Batman. "That's not the behavior of worshiping a queen."

The group of them didn't move from their position of heads to the ground. I motioned for Lila to come to me and she flew to my shoulder. I agreed with him, this felt hinky.

I took a few steps back. "But it is the behavior of those who might think they can control a queen. And use her power over the other dragons." I put a boot to one of the red-robed creatures and pushed him over. He didn't fight me, but instead stared up at me from his back. "That about right, you little jerk?"

He closed his eyes and shook his head rapidly. "Please don't kill me. I do only as my mistress bids. She asked us to bring the little queen to her. That is the goal, no harm is meant."

The others gasped and they went to their hands and knees. Hands grabbed at him and dragged him across the ground. They spoke in that weird whispering echo and it rapidly spread through the pack of them.

"You aren't supposed to speak. That's the priest's job." The words rebounded around us as they took him down.

His bulbous blue eyes were frantic as he tried to push them off. "Save me, I'll tell you anything I can! Please!"

The screech that went up from the remaining red-robed ding-dongs was ear-piercing, but I didn't let it slow me down. I bolted toward them, shifting forms mid-stride. Sure, a six-pound house cat didn't sound fierce until it's slicing your face into ribbons with claws that were sharper and stronger than they had any right to be.

I launched onto the back of the ding-dong closest to me, dug all four sets of claws in deep until he screeched and writhed to get away from me, then bounded across to the next. Maks waded in with his bladed spear and one head rolled off, the blood not even showing against the red robes.

"Grab him!" I yelled at Maks.

Lila looped above us and spit out a mouthful of acid.

If I thought the screams from my claws were something, it was nothing to the screams from her acid as it burned right through them, cutting them down before they could come at us.

Maks scooped up the defector under one arm and ran back to the horses. I ran after them, shifting back to two legs as I leapt onto Balder's back. Lila barrel rolled past us and dove into the sand to remove the last of the acid from her lips.

The screams of those red-robed little creatures echoed across the desert landscape, and if I knew anything, it was that screams brought out the worst of the supernatural world looking for a quick and easy meal. "Lila, hurry, we gotta go."

The last thing I wanted was a run-in with something bigger than us, something stronger, or with more magic. Which, at that particular moment, was pretty much anything in the supernatural world.

I held Balder back waiting for her, letting Batman and Maks get ahead of us, knowing we could catch them. Lila burst out of a sand pile and shook off the loose grains as she flew toward me. I barely waited for her to grab hold of the back of the saddle before I urged Balder to go.

The pounding of hoofbeats under me, the wind in my ears, and I could still hear the screams of the red-robed ones behind us. The minutes ticked by as we galloped away as fast as we could through the loose sand. Balder loved it, his neck stretched out and his ears pricked forward as he picked up speed with each stride.

The screams faded in the distance until there was finally nothing. Maks pulled up first and Batman let out a low snort.

The little red-robed man, creature, whatever he was, sat in front of Maks. The little guy was shaking hard and stunned by what had happened.

"What are you?" I asked. Rude in our world, but whatever. I was already known for not having much tact. The east might as well get used to it.

He turned his head to me. "My name is Insha. I am of clan Tuvok. We are ghouls. I did not mean for you to kill them." He looked back the way we'd come. "My mistress will not be happy with me."

I wrinkled my nose up. I'd heard of ghouls but hadn't had much dealings with them. They had very little magic and worked like ants, using sheer numbers to overwhelm their intended prey. "Scavengers then. Are there more ghouls around here?"

He shook his head rapidly. "No, most ghouls have been scattered, the clans broken and mixed, so there is no true loyalty now except to our mistress, may she forever grace us with her presence and beauty."

I looked at Maks. His eyes were thoughtful and rested heavily on the head of the ghoul sitting in front of him. I wondered who this mistress was but let the question slide for the moment. We had more pressing issues than a ghoul's love affair with a woman.

"Ghouls are a distant cousin to the Jinn," Maks said. "But with less magic, and the same connection to the sands. Minor abilities in glamor and mind control."

Insha bobbed his head, his enormous eyes blinking under the heat of the sun. "Yes, that is true. But we have no dealings with the Jinn, not since the forbidding happened."

My eyebrows shot up. "Lila, you think you can find us a place to take shelter for a few hours?"

Insha twisted suddenly, pointing straight east. "A mile that way, and we'll come upon a shelter we could use within the rock valleys, an old structure that is safe from the others that lurk in these lands."

He didn't seem to notice that his sharp movement had made Maks pull a knife and place the point directly against his upper spine.

Slowly Maks put the knife away when it was apparent that the ghoul was oblivious and just giving us a direction to follow.

I looked from Maks to Lila and then back again. They each gave a quick nod. There was no reason to think that our new companion was up to something. He'd wanted to be free of the other ghouls, and now we needed shelter.

More was our bad for trusting the little jerk.

"All right," I said, "let's go."

We started out again at a brisk walk, all four of us silent. My mind raced with what I did know about ghouls—which wasn't a great deal. And what the hell was this *forbidding* he was talking about? Who had made the forbidding? And why against Jinn?

Lila crawled over my shoulder and whispered quietly, "Wanna bet the Beast from the East has something to do with this?"

I snorted. "I'd not bet against you, that's for sure." Because like Lila, I thought the same thing.

We'd barely stepped foot toward the east, and our welcome had been set out.

If only we understood how very wrong we were about what we were up against, we might just have gone running the other way.

## 5

Insha, a cherub who I was sure wasn't, was correct in his directions to the east. He led us into a valley of naturally made standing rocks curved in the middle with wide flat tops. For a moment, I worried they would have some connection to a higher power as had those that I'd encountered in the past, but they were just rocks that had been carved away by time, wind, and water. I reached up and touched one of the red stone formations as we rode under it. The rock just a rock, smooth in some places and rough in others.

"We are almost there," Insha chirped excitedly. "Safety is a boon in this place where the desert meets the mountains and the jungle."

"He talks weird," Lila muttered, gripping the

front of my saddle hard enough to make it creak. "I don't trust him."

"We aren't trusting him, not really," I said. "Just letting him lead us through a maze of rocks to a place we don't know while believing he is telling us the truth. That's hardly trust."

She shot me a look, her eyebrows dipping low over her violet eyes. "Don't be saucy with me. You know what I mean. This whole thing gives me the heebie-jeebies."

I sighed, agreeing. Also knowing that we needed a place to rest. "If there is anything dodgy about it, we'll leave right away, and we'll leave him behind. Okay?"

Lila tucked her wings tightly to her body and shivered. "Yeah, okay."

We wove our way deeper into the canyon of rocks, the formations towering over our heads. Barren, desolate, empty of life.

Maks rode a little ahead of us, Insha chattering away quietly enough that even I couldn't hear the words though the tone was pleasant enough. Excited. Happy.

I felt the pull to go closer, to bend my head and listen to whatever it was Insha wanted to tell me. Crap. Was he putting Maks under some sort of spell?

"Maks," I said, "look at me."

He slowly turned his head and lifted an eyebrow. "What?"

I stared hard into his eyes, and they were as clear and blue as any other day. "Never mind, getting my knickers in a knot."

That was all I got to say because we rounded another formation and ahead of us was a stone castle. There was no other word for it. Circular, the castle was a single turret, easily three hundred feet across and the same in height if I were to guess.

The structure sat at the intersection of two roads running the cardinal directions. "Anyone else seeing the similarities to the crossroads?" I muttered.

Lila squeaked. "Yes, too much."

I blinked and saw movement in the windows and then a flurry of little red-robed ghouls came rushing out of the castle toward us.

Maks twisted in his saddle as Insha slid off to the ground. "What do you think? Do we stay? Or do we go?"

I watched as Insha was welcomed by his fellow ghouls, all of them excitedly smacking him on the back, then finally lifting him over their heads as if he were a returning hero and not a survivor of his group being slaughtered. I mean . . . the behavior was strange at best, and it gave me a shiver of apprehension.

"You aren't under some sort of spell?" I asked. "He was talking away. I couldn't hear what he was saying."

Maks winked at me. "I'm just a human to him. He wasn't trying to spell me, but convince me that he was to be trusted, and that he was one of the good ghouls." He paused and edged Batman closer to me so he could scoop up my hand. "Not everyone is out to get us, Zam. Sometimes people are just what they say they are. He spoke of the Jinn, and not in a good light, so let's keep that part quiet for now."

I grimaced. "Fair, but sometimes people are liars and thieves and they really are out to get us."

Lila grunted. "I agree with both of you. So, which is it?"

I made myself get off Balder but kept close to him. "No matter what, we don't let them separate us from the horses, even if it means sleeping in a stable," I said.

Just in case I was right, and Maks was wrong, I wanted a quick escape. I didn't see any other live-stock that could be ridden; drawing close to the circular castle, I saw only a few goats and a scattering of chickens around the side of the structure. There was no scent of animals, just the ever-present heat and the aroma of hot sand. Which, yes, does have a smell all its own.

The lack of other horses or anything that could be ridden was good. It meant there would be no chase to speak of should we have to make a go of it and leave in a hurry.

Lila crawled closer to me, up onto my shoulder, and dropped down my back a little. I pulled my hood up and she cowered inside it. "I hate feeling vulnerable again. It's almost worse than before," she said softly.

I reached back and touched her on top of the head. "We're together, it will be okay, Lila. We'll figure this out." Yes, I was repeating myself, but she needed to hear the words again.

I knew exactly what she was feeling. For just a moment, we all had enough strength that we felt like we could face anything that came our way, and then . . . that rug was yanked out from under us like a flying magic carpet.

The red-robed ghouls danced and cavorted, singing in a language I didn't know, across what was, I assumed, the courtyard of the circular castle. They chanted and sang, their words tumbling over one another yet still sounding melodic despite the strangeness of their language.

"You getting any of this?" I asked Maks under my breath.

"Nope. I don't speak Ghoulish," he said. "And

none of my memories show any interaction with them."

It took a solid ten minutes of dancing and chanting for the little buggers to slow themselves enough to put Insha on the ground. He waved us forward with both hands, wiggling his fingers. "Come inside, come inside!"

The other ghouls stepped to either side, creating a channel for us to walk down.

Lila shivered against my back. "Creepy."

"Creepy doesn't mean evil," I said, but even I didn't believe my own words. "That being said," I swung back up onto Balder's back, "thank you, but no. We'll pass."

Maks didn't question me and Lila breathed out a sigh of relief. "Thank you. I don't like it here. There is a feeling of . . . anticipation that is crawling around my head."

For me, it wasn't a matter of like or dislike so much as it was recognizing that we didn't have a leg to stand on if we went into the structure. We'd be trapped with a single door shutting behind us and no way to easily get out.

I turned Balder around, heading back the way we'd ridden in, and my breath caught in my throat as I stared at the image in front of us.

The circular castle was—impossibly—right there. I looked over my shoulder to see the castle behind us, then to the front again where it also sat.

I spun Balder and put my heels to his sides, driving him down the western road, only to pull up short in two strides as the castle sat like a lump of stone that was not going to be denied.

"It won't matter which road you take, the lady of the house would speak with you," Insha said. "And she will not let you leave until you speak with her. This is one of her skills."

Lila's claws dug into my neck. "This is not good. No one who forces your hand is a good person."

I looked at Maks. His face was tight with anger and worry, no doubt a mirror of my own emotions that rolled through me.

"I don't like games, Insha," I growled and forced myself off Balder. Balder bumped my back with his nose, pushing me forward.

Insha smiled, flashing some seriously sharp teeth. "But cats love games; they love to play with those they kill first, not unlike ghouls."

Maks pulled his staff, the blade at the end wickedly sharp as it rested just in the hollow of Insha's throat. "We are leaving now."

"She will not care if I die," Insha said. "There are many to replace me as you saw in the desert where you came upon us. I suggest you speak with her, and if you are brave and smart, you might get what you came for. Or you might get more than you came for."

"You brought us here, you can take us out," I growled, feeling the jungle cat under my skin all but begging to be let loose on the little bastard. To claw and tear my way through his body and make a damn example of him.

He spread his hands wide. "I cannot. I am a slave to the mistress, gladly a slave for she protects us from Asag and his army." He bowed at the waist and made a sign with one hand, pressing it to his forehead. Circling his finger to his thumb, the rest of his fingers spread outward, as if they were shading his face.

The creaking of well-oiled but old hinges whispered through the dry desert air.

"Insha, you may all go to your homes now." Her voice was deep and thrummed through me, a pounding in my chest. Her words were wrapped in magic and they reverberated in my bones.

The ghouls didn't scatter, but sunk into the ground, leaving behind puddles of their robes from where they'd been standing.

I locked my eyes on the lady of the house.

Her black hair had a single streak of white on either side of her head, starting at the temple. She wore it long, loose, flowing all the way to her knees.

Her dress was silk and dyed the deepest red, a color so dark that it bordered on black. It did not cling to her curves, and yet as she moved you could clearly see how feminine she was with the sway of her hips.

She was perhaps in her middle forties, her face heart-shaped and girlish despite her age. Eyes the color of honey stared at me. There was no hate in them, no anger, just . . . curiosity.

"How interesting to finally meet you, Zamira, the Desert Cursed. And you, Lila, queen of the dragons." Her eyes swept to Maks and quickly dismissed him. "And your human mate, Zamira. I'd heard that you were bedding a Jinn master, but this one looks like a shifter to me." That deep thrumming voice echoed in my chest and I grimaced.

"Can't say the same for you," I said. "What are you? And what do you want from us?"

Again, interminably rude, but I was not about to treat her with any sort of respect when she had tricked us to bring us here. Games were the shits, and I hated them.

She clasped her hands in front of her body. "There is payment for passage into the lands that I hold. And if I understand correctly, you seek out the hatchlings of Dragon's Ground. You seek passage into Asag's lands to find them?"

Damn it, how did she know? I wasn't good at schooling my face and she laughed at me.

"Your deeds and battles have reached even us, here in the lands cut off from your own desert. Whispers of a rider known for her cunning and ability to find the most treacherous of items. Of the jewels of power and of other things." She paused, her eyes sweeping over us. "A rider who befriends those who have no magic of their own and yet she shows them a new way to survive."

Her hands spread wide like Insha had done, yet on her it looked elegant and graceful. "I will answer your questions, as I am sure you have many, but you must come inside. The heat does not agree with me."

I highly doubted that. She lived in the middle of blasted desert. There was no way the heat bothered her all that much. I looked at Maks. He gave the subtlest of nods. Because, like me, he already knew the answer.

We had no choice. We had no magic with which to compel her, so that meant, at the moment, we were doing what she wanted. And there was no easy road away from this place. We had to play by her rules.

Lila gave a low growl. "I hate this."

"You and me both." I breathed the words as I

slid off Balder's back. Again. I touched his nose and whispered softly to him, "Be ready."

He snorted, bobbed his head and pawed at the ground.

The question was, what was he to be ready for? We couldn't get away, but even so, I felt like I'd be a fool not to acknowledge that what was happening here was a shit deal. That I wanted us all to be ready for whatever was coming. If there was a chance to escape and make a run for it, we would take it.

Maks stepped up beside me, his arm brushing mine, the back of his hand bumping my own. He wouldn't take my hand; that would show too much to this new threat.

"Into the deep," he muttered.

I drew a breath and made myself walk to where I stood only a few feet away from this new person. "You know my name, you know Lila's and you know Maks's. But we don't know yours."

She smiled, perfect white teeth flashing against her dark skin. "I am Mamitu, desert born, and desert cursed." She dipped her head toward me. "Just like you."

## 6

Mamitu's words rang hard in my ears. Desert born, desert cursed. She was like me? Part Jinn, part shifter, part fairy, part whatever else got tossed into my bloodline?

She motioned for us to follow her through the doorway into the castle. "Come, I will explain as much as I can to you with the time allotted."

That alone pulled me forward, my curiosity something that unfortunately got the better of me on more than one occasion. What time? Who was timing us? Because it sounded like it wasn't her idea. Maks fell in behind me, his breathing hitched as if he were struggling to get enough air. "Tread lightly," he said quietly.

Mamitu led us to the center of the castle, a

massive courtyard filled with trees, grass, a bubbling spring, and a cool breeze that did not belong in the desert. This was heavy magic here, though it did not feel dangerous.

"Come, rest yourselves." She snapped her fingers and the sun dimmed a little. The thump of hooves on hard ground rumbled behind us and Balder and Batman trotted into the open space. She'd beckoned them?

"I know what he is," she said softly, her eyes landing lightly on Balder. "One of the last. There are perhaps a dozen left in the world. And yet he is bonded to you as surely as if you were his own species."

Balder stared at her a moment and then dropped his head to graze. I forced myself to take off his saddle and bridle. He dropped to the sweet grasses and rolled. Batman followed his lead after Maks removed his gear.

Lila shot out from under my hood. "Why are you being nice? First your little red assholes attack us, then you make it so we can't leave, and now this, acting like we are friends? You are not fooling me!"

Mamitu pressed her palms together and bent over them. "I admit, perhaps how I brought you here was not the best of ways, but I have little ability to affect the world around us. Not like I once did. And the eyes of others watch me closely. I must follow their rules. Here, though, he cannot see me. I had to make it look like I was taking you to harm you, for fear of bringing down his wrath."

"You mean this Asag you mentioned?" Maks asked.

She gave a terse nod. "Yes. He is why I am here. He is why I must bring travelers to my keep. Once inside these walls, though, his eyes cannot pierce the stone."

Maks and I shared a quick look behind her back as she led the way. This Asag sounded like a major dick. Already I knew in my gut that he would be the one we had to deal with, and no doubt was the Beast from the East the hyena shifter had spoken of. But was he the one with the hatchlings?

"You said you were desert born, desert cursed. So are you Jinn? Or a shifter?" We found ourselves following her deeper into the stunning courtyard. I was mesmerized by the beauty, smells, and feeling of utter serenity that flowed through as clearly as the water in the creek, all of which made me seriously suspicious. Trees covered in fruit and flowering blooms littered the place, giving shade, and the air was cool and refreshing.

I did not believe she was a Jinn or a shifter or

some combination of the two; she didn't smell like either. I just wanted to see what she answered.

Mamitu lowered herself to a wooden carved seat by a bend in the flow of water, a smoothly planed table beside her where she rested one arm. "I am desert born, a goddess of sorts, not unlike your Ishtar."

All the good feelings, all the serenity fled in a flush of anger and residual pain that came with that name. All the lies, all the love that was destroyed for Ishtar's quest to rule, to have all the power once more.

Maks cleared his throat. "That name will not endear you to any of us, but most especially not to Zam."

She waved a hand. "I mean only that I have the power of this desert in my veins, and was born many, many years ago. Goddess is a term that is used far more lightly here than in the west. Perhaps mage would be better. I have abilities that make me strong, and they are tied to the desert."

"You mean like Merlin?" Lila queried. "That comparison will not help you either."

Mamitu sighed. "Many with power are foolish and dangerous with it. I will agree with you on that count. Merlin was one of the worst. Like a spoiled child whose parents had too much money and not enough sense to bless him with a work ethic and understanding that with so much power there should be a heavy burden of responsibility."

My lips twitched at the analogy. I did not want to like her. "Why are you forcing us here then? If you aren't like them?"

Her smile was not quite as soft as before. "You wish to cross my eastern mountains in search of the hatchlings, yes?"

I nodded. "Yes."

"Then you need my permission and my mark. Any who try to cross without those, die. The rhuks of the mountains tear them apart before they can pass. Of course, if the western deserts hadn't cut themselves off from the rest of us, you would know these things." Mamitu spread her hands on her skirts, smoothing the material. "Before you ask, let me explain fully. I do not like to half-ass things."

Yeah, I liked her a little better now that she'd cussed. Stupid, but it was the truth.

"The eastern portion of our piece of this world is ruled by Asag, whose name you have heard now. He is in the center of the east if you must know, and where the hatchlings are taken. But you will not reach him until you go through my land, and through the land of Pazuzu. Asag has bound us to protect him, clever demon that he is."

"Demon?" Lila blurted out. "What do you mean, *demon*?"

"Hush, little one," Mamitu cooed. "He is a demon of the underworld, like any other demon. Only he has found ways to gain power—like Ishtar. Like Merlin."

My heart started beating all too hard in my chest. "You mean he found the stones of power?"

"No, those you dealt with and they will remain as they are for centuries to come." She waved a hand. "But there are other ways to gain power. Stealing the hatchlings is one. Stealing the magic of others is another." Her eyes rested on each of us. She knew then that we'd been stripped of our abilities. "And the last is his army."

"So, he's a thief," Maks said.

"Yes." Mamitu gave a brief nod. "And I believe it will take a thief to stop him. All who have come before you have great powers, great size, muscles and weapons bristling upon their bodies. They come in a force that they believe is great enough to stop Asag. But perhaps it would take one not so large to find their way to the center of his holdings." Her eyes swept to me again and I grimaced but kept my mouth shut. I wasn't going to throw myself on the sword if I didn't have to. "I knew Lila would be the marker by which to be certain I brought the right rider into my home. That is why the ghouls trapped her first. A small dragon is not common."

We were there to rescue the hatchlings, a promise I'd made what seemed a lifetime ago to the mothers distraught at the loss of their children.

I had not banked on there being a battle of armies and demons involved.

Mamitu bobbed her head several times. "Yes, I believe that you might be able to do what others could not, Zamira. Then again, the three of you might die on the first of this journey. Both paths are possible. I have seen them in vision and dreams. Many paths, many choices."

Lila gripped my shoulder hard. "So to save the hatchlings, we must take down this Asag demon?"

Our hostess nodded. "Yes, and by the rules of the land that Asag has tied me to, you must first gain permission to pass through my lands."

That seemed easy enough. "May we have your permission to cross your lands?" I asked.

Mamitu smiled, sad but still smiling. "You may ask, and when the task given to you has been completed, my mark of safety you will wear. Then you shall pass by the winged rhuk unnoticed."

I closed my eyes, already knowing this was part of the game. "A task. Has anyone completed it before?"

Sure, I already knew the answer, too, because that was how my life went. Desert born, desert cursed.

"No one has ever completed the task I would lay before you," she said softly. "This is the riddle that Asag has created to keep himself safe. To keep his armies growing and all of us underfoot. He is clever and he is deadly, and unlike many demons, he is patient."

"He wants to take over the world?" Maks asked. "Like the Emperor and Merlin?"

Mamitu shook a finger and her head at the same time. "No, he is rather lazy, also a demonic trait. Ruling the world would be too much for him. But in that laziness, he is vicious about protecting what he perceives as his. And now that the Emperor, Ishtar, and Merlin are no longer in play, he will expand his reach, putting another care-taker in place that would protect him on his throne. He will create another layer of protection to keep the lands that are his safe."

A lazy demon? Awesome.

"Let me get this straight." I held up one hand in a full-stop position. "You are somehow in thrall to this Asag, and he forces you to protect him in the outer ring of his territory." I pointed to us. "We then have to complete a task in order to pass, and then the next protector is Pazuzu, who I assume will also have a task for us that has never been challenged even once since no one has passed your task?" I paused and shook my head as

I gathered the last of my thoughts. "Sound about right?"

She nodded. "Yes, that is the right of it."

I drew a breath, trying not to be hasty. "What do you gain if we take him down?"

Her eyes widened and she put a hand to her chest, her fingers splayed wide. "Wait, do you believe you could *kill* Asag? He has stripped you of your abilities, he has stripped you of all the strength that he could, and you still think that you could end his reign? I thought only that you would free the hatchlings and hurt his power structure."

I shrugged. "We've faced bad odds before."

"These are not just bad odds," she said. "The task that you must complete is not one that I set out, but that Asag has set. It . . . is impossible." She breathed out the words, her face twisting with obvious pain. "And I say that with difficulty because of the bindings that he has put on me."

Her words were truthful as far as I could tell, and while I was not perfect at reading people, I'd gotten better at it. "The ghouls?"

"His. They are as much my guards as I am their master. I told them that I desired a small dragon of my own. To give to Asag. They are mostly rather dull in the head and believed it. With the exception of Insha; he is loyal to me and I trust him."

That right there made me nervous. To trust

one of your enemies set to guard you seemed a foolish thing to me. Okay, it was fucking stupid, not just foolish.

Maks had been quiet through much of this; he finally spoke. "And you knew we were coming, because of your own abilities?"

She startled and looked at him anew. "What do you know of me, human male?"

He kept his blue eyes looking downward. "Mamitu, goddess of fate and destiny, of oaths and occasionally irrevocable curses. You saw us in a line of fate, a potential destiny that could free you, did you? How many others have you seen with such potential?"

I watched the interplay between the two of them, and how very suddenly she was interested in Maks after she'd so simply dismissed him. "What magic did Asag take from you?"

"I am a mage of sorts." He bowed at the waist.

Her eyebrows shot up. "And he took *all* your abilities? Sweet holy sepulcher. He is gaining in strength then. With mages, he often can only take one aspect of their power, not all of it." She pressed her fingers together and a sigh escaped her. "Yes, I saw that some of you have potential, but I also see many ways in which you each die on this journey. Still, there is a spark in each of you that has defied fate more than once, and so I ask, why not again?

The lines of your lives are interwoven, and I see many changes for you. Especially you, Lila."

Lila put the tip of one claw to her chest. "Me? Why me?"

"The love of your life draws closer, but I doubt you will see him, or him you." She shrugged. "I am sorry, I cannot tell you more than that, I only see that your true mate is nigh at hand."

Lila's jaw hung open. "Well, that's a shitty way to explain it!"

Mamitu smiled and then the smile fled. "The question still remains. Will you take the task I offer you? To gain my protection and permission to cross the mountains into Pazuzu's territory? To find your way through the east to the heart of our world?"

I could feel Maks's hesitation and my own matched it. "You're sure there is no other way to breach Asag's territory?"

Mamitu shook her head. "There is not. You either go the way the path decrees, or you die here at the hands of the ghouls."

"We might die anyway," Lila said. "And before I can even meet the love of my life, apparently."

I didn't miss the sarcasm or the hint of hope that flared in her. That connection between us was still there, that ability to sense strong emotions when we were close by each other. I reached up and touched a hand to her back, smoothing down her wings.

"Basically, we have no choice. That is what you're saying?" I said. "We either take this task you offer us, or we die right now?"

Mamitu nodded. "You have the right of it."

I blew out a slow breath and looked at Maks. His eyes spoke volumes. There was no choice, so we might as well agree to her terms. Unless . . .

"What is the task that you would lay at our feet?" Yeah, I was feeling particularly proper in that moment.

Mamitu spread her hand out over the creek beside her and the water spilled upward, pooling in the air in front of her like a mirror. I found myself stepping closer to see what she would show us within the water.

There was a slab of rock, and then the slab was buried under mounds of sand, and then that sand was covered with water. The image spilled upward as if we were thrown into the air and my stomach lurched at the sudden change of imagery. I took in the landscape around the river. A rock shaped like a pair of wings sat to the west along a mountain with the tip broken clean off.

Mamitu swirled her fingers through the water and the image changed to a gold container with a handle on either side. Glyphs were carved deep into the gold, symbols that made my skin crawl and my heart whisper. They were not much different than the language of the Jinn. Jinn, but darker.

Far more deadly.

"The Vessel of Vahab," Mamitu said. "Bring it to me, and you will have safety as you cross through my lands to the throne of Pazuzu."

## 7

**M**amitu, the goddess or mage in a godforsaken desert castle, swirled her hands through the water and the droplets fell at our feet, soaking into the thick grass of the courtyard. "You may stay here a night and rest yourselves. But at the cock's crow, you must leave or your lives will be forfeit. I have told you all I can, and so I bid you goodnight, and may whatever gods you worship see your feet safely to your destination."

She stood and walked between us, away from the courtyard to a door covered with crawling green plants.

The three of us watched her go and the silence between us was heavy. Maks was the one to finally break it. "Well, this should be fun."

I went to him and circled my arms around his waist and leaned my head against his chest. "Nothing is ever going to be easy, is it?"

"For some it isn't," he said, then kissed me on top of my head. "I mean, you just got the luck of the draw, right?"

I shot him a look and caught the edge of his smile before it slid away. "Bet you're wishing you'd stayed with Nell now, aren't you?"

"Gods no." He lowered himself to the grass and lay flat out. "She was interminably boring. Nothing ever happened. She didn't like to put herself into danger's oncoming path. How could I have lived with that tedious boredom without going crazy?"

Lila swooped down from my shoulder and hopped across to him. "Toad. Did you hear what she said about me? How could I not recognize the love of my life? What does she mean by that?"

I had an idea, but I wasn't sure that Lila would like what I had to say.

Which meant I said it anyway. "What if he wasn't the same species? I almost missed out on Maks because at first he was nothing but a dirty grubby human, and then worse, he was a dirty filthy . . . mage." I didn't know why he hadn't told Mamitu he was Jinn, but I wasn't going to out him. If he felt like he couldn't be honest with Mamitu about that portion of his life, I wouldn't tell her either.

"Thank you. I do always feel the depth of your love when you speak of me." Maks flung an arm over his eyes, but he was smiling. Our path might not have been straight, but it was true and honest. I wouldn't trade it for the world.

"Another species? But that's a *terrible* idea!" she barked and hopped around on the grass, clearly agitated by this bit of news, her wings stretched out and shaking, claws digging deep into the soft ground over and over again. Never mind that we were likely going to die a terrible death on a hunt for some stupid item we'd never get to—she was worried about her love life.

Yet, despite the danger ahead, I didn't feel fatigued or upset, I was . . . well, I was excited to go for it. "I think there is something wrong with me." I lay down beside Maks. "I should be upset, at the very least. Shouldn't I? Freaked out that we're going to walk onto a path of certain danger and possible death?"

"You excited too?" Maks asked.

I rolled over so my body was half on top of his. Lila made a gagging noise. "Get a tent, you two."

I ignored her. "I think something might be wrong with *us* then. You know that, right? We shouldn't be excited to face our deaths again. Especially so soon after the last few rounds. Especially with a demon involved that we know very little about."

He snorted and slid an arm around my waist. "You've been doing this for years, though. You were searching out the gems for Ishtar, honing your skills and going against supernaturals that were far out of your league in terms of power. Witches. Giants. Shifters. You've been stealing things right out from under their owners' noses. You do remember Dragon's Ground, don't you?"

I tapped a finger on his chest. "That is what brought us here, so yes, I do happen to recall our brief stay in Dragon's Ground." I paused, my thoughts circling around and around like a murder of crows. "There is always something more, something just out on the edge of the horizon pulling us out of our comfort zones. What if this time, we don't come back from the pull? What if this is the time that . . . one of us dies?"

Because while I wasn't worried about my own life, the idea that Maks or Lila could be hurt was almost too much to bear. I could face anything in this world with the two of them at my side.

They were my greatest strengths and my greatest weaknesses. I knew it. They knew it. I was worried that Asag, this new threat, would know it too.

I laid my head on Maks's chest and listened to his heartbeat. The steady thump under my ear eased some of my worries and I let myself drift off, knowing that he was there. We'd learned when to rest when we could, and this was one of those times. There was no point in staying awake, not when it was obvious that our hostess was bent on sending us after some stupidly dangerous artifact. She wasn't going to kill us now. Not when something or someone else would likely do the job for her.

Lila dropped onto the two of us and pushed her way in between our bodies, grumbling about wanting to get in on the cuddling too. I draped an arm over her and let my mind settle.

What I didn't expect was the dreamscape to flow over me.

A world beyond the waking one that had shattered, broken when the Emperor was defeated, and his power stripped. It shouldn't have been where I opened my eyes, not in the least.

I blinked, not sure at first if what I was seeing was the waking world. I was in the same courtyard as my sleeping body. I stood and Lila groaned. Maks was not there, but I could see Balder and Batman grazing across from us. Not everyone could walk the dreamscape. Lila had come with me more than once.

"No, no, this place isn't supposed to exist anymore. What the hell is going on?" She stumbled away from where Maks slept in the real world, unaware that our dreams were far different from his.

"Well, I guess it means we can do some snooping." I headed straight for the door that Mamitu had slid through, opened it, and stepped into a well-lit corridor. Lila flew to my shoulder and landed lightly, using my ear to balance herself. "Even if we don't know why it's here."

I shut the door behind us and followed my nose, picking up the smell of fresh growing things —something that I'd not noticed on Mamitu. Of course, she'd been surrounded by all the greenery and I'd assumed that had been what I was smelling.

Clinging to the edges of the hallway, I followed the scent up three flights to the rooftop of the circular castle. A ring castle in truth. On the rooftop, the wind blew hotter, drier, the desert doing its thing and making me yearn for the sands we'd left behind.

Voices called back and forth.

I crept forward. There were others in this dream world then, and that was interesting in and of itself. Few could walk the dreamscape, yet I could hear at least four other voices. I tucked myself behind a parapet and did a quick look around. Four people. Two men I didn't recognize, Mamitu, and Insha, the little ghoul.

"They are set on going after the Vessel of Vahab," Mamitu said.

Insha bobbed his head. "Good. They will be the ones, if any, to get us out of this hole we are sunk in."

Mamitu sighed. "But so we thought of the others too. How many have died trying to work their way through the paths of the riddle that Asag has made? The paths we are all forced to follow?"

The shorter of the two men with a dark, crisply trimmed beard stroked his hands over his face. "You have warned them with all that you can. They seek the hatchlings, yes?" Mamitu nodded and he went on. "A noble cause, and one worth championing where we can. Will you give the girl a weapon?"

That perked my ears up. A weapon was exactly what I needed.

The taller of the two men snorted. He had the look of the shorter, only with no beard. Related for sure, if I were to guess. "Pazuzu, you are stupid if you believe that. If we so much as lift a finger to help them, we will be found out that we are trying to stop Asag. These three will die, as did all the others, and I will not go down with them. As it is, we can barely keep Asag happy. I have sent him another harem as he is already done with the last."

"Brother," Pazuzu said, confirming my thoughts, "we know you are in his inner circle. That you are in the most danger should any plan go awry. Let us see what these three can do. If they can bring the Vessel of Vahab to Mamitu, then we must decide from there. Until they do that, we can give them no help."

The taller man grimaced, turned away, and disappeared.

Insha slumped and also disappeared, leaving only Mamitu and Pazuzu. "What do you think of them?" he asked softly. "Will they survive? You have seen their fate, their destiny as clearly as you see all the others."

Mamitu turned from him and I ducked back behind the parapet.

"They . . . they might survive," she said. "Their fellowship is strong, and they have faced great hardships before, but always with a little aid here and there. With magic and strength that Asag has now stripped from them. The Beast has always been wary of those who would cross into his boundary, and this time is not any different. His reach is spreading. He will take more power if he is not stopped soon."

"Might?" Pazuzu said. "Might survive. Of all

those who have gone before, none even had a slight chance, and you tried to stop them all."

Mamitu was quiet but for the rustling of her skirts. "The dragon will survive. The cat will survive. The other . . . his fate is darkest of them all and the one most likely to die. A mage stripped of his powers indeed."

Pazuzu breathed out a sigh. "To lose one, though, to lose one and have the others succeed! That is a great hope, Mamitu. Why did you not say this before?"

"Because I had to be certain of what I was seeing," she said. "Each choice a soul makes changes the path they walk. As soon as the cat decided she was going to take this challenge, it solidified this particular line of fate."

I closed my eyes, my chest tight with a fear that I knew right to the soles of my feet. Lila's claws dug into me, but the pain was welcome. It matched the pain in my heart.

Maks would die if we went onward. We all would die if we stayed.

"You will let her choose a weapon?" Pazuzu asked again.

"I will," Mamitu said. "Now, please leave me, I have things I must attend to."

Pazuzu was the one I would go to next if I could face off against the challenge Mamitu gave me.

I stood and faced Mamitu. Her eyes were on me already as if she knew I'd been there. "You heard."

"Yes. Did you know I was there?"

She shook her head. "Not right away, but then I felt your choice waver and knew that you were hearing me. Dreamwalking is not so easy a talent. But you are the Emperor's granddaughter, and he has given you that gift."

"The dreamscape broke when his power was taken," I said. "How is this possible?"

She nodded slowly. "Yes, his hold on the dreamscape slid, but there are always dreams with which to wander through. He is not the creator of dreams, even you cannot believe that? The dream-scape is larger than any one person."

Yes, we were both avoiding the obvious, the thing most heavy on my heart and mind.

"Is Maks going to die?" Lila burst off my shoulder. "Is he?"

Mamitu's eyes swept downward. "His death would be certain if he was to go with you. He would die to save one of you, that is what I see. Let me show you."

She reached out and touched my hand, and the world wobbled around us.

No longer in the castle keep of Mamitu, I had a

hard time recognizing the new landscape. But I knew the man.

Maks stood in front of me, a blade buried deeply in his belly. His hands cupped the weapon as he slowly lifted his eyes to mine and whispered my name.

The image changed and again it was Maks, only this time his body was covered in wounds that could only be strange bites. He lay on the ground, seizing as the breath rattled out of him, heavy green foliage all around him.

And again. His body dissolving in front of my eyes as if Lila's acid rained down on him, liquifying him as I was unable to look away, his eyes the last thing to fade as he again whispered my name, the last thing he said as death took him.

"ENOUGH!" I yelled and snapped myself back to the present moment. "Enough."

"If he survives one, there are too many other paths for him to die on," Mamitu said. "I am sorry."

Lila let out a cry, but I said nothing, my heart and mind racing through all the possibilities. I would not let him die, not after all I'd done to keep him with me.

"You're sure." Yes, I asked even though I'd seen the visions. I knew better than any other that visions could be twisted and changed to fit your needs, yet at the same time there was a solid truth about these I could not deny, though I was trying for all I was worth to do just that.

"I am rarely if ever wrong," she said. "All the others who have gone before you were destined to die. You . . . there is something about you and the dragon that is different. You are touched by some power I do not recognize. It has given you a strength and understanding rarely gifted to those who have lived such a short time as yourselves. The armies that have come before you to face Asag were huge, full of power and strength. Cunning is what you need to survive this task, cunning and the willingness to bend. The willingness to use your mind and not just the strength of your sword arm."

I closed my eyes, hearing her words, and understanding in my heart that she was not playing us false. It was in her best interest for us to survive, for us to bring her the Vessel of Vahab.

"You would question me, yes?" she asked. "You would wonder if I am being honest with you?"

"No," I said. "I don't trust you, but I don't think you are lying. The dreamscape has a tendency to make people more open than they would be otherwise."

She tipped her head to me. "Then you must go without him. But before you leave, come to the chamber on the western side of the castle. You need a weapon to see you through this."

Her words rippled through the air. But all I could think was that Maks would die if he came with us on this journey.

"He'll follow us, if we leave without him," I said. "What happens then?"

"He may live if he follows you, but if he rides out with you, then his death is certain. I cannot stop him. You understand that is not my role. In that my hands are tied."

I tipped my head. "You won't have to stop him."

I looked at Lila and she nodded. "We will."

## 8

I woke up from the dreamscape but held very still. Maks's arm was around me as we slept on the grass in the castle's keep. He slept soundly, almost as if he were spelled. I didn't care in that moment, only happy that he did not wake with me. Maks awake would make this leave-taking all that much more difficult. Lila peered up from where she snuggled between our bodies.

Mamitu's words hung heavily in my mind and heart. I could have chosen not to believe her, but Maks himself had said she was a goddess of destiny and fate. And there was no reason for her to speak freely with the others she was meeting, other than to tell them the truth. None of them had known Lila and I were listening.

There were times to believe, and times not to. This was of the former.

I shifted my weight and Maks stirred. I pressed a hand to his chest. "I'm just going to check on the horses," I said softly.

He mumbled something; I leaned over and kissed him. A smile spread over his mouth, his lips moving against mine. I managed to keep my tears back and just kissed him harder. "I love you, Maks."

"Love you," he whispered and let me go, his hand sliding off my body, over my hip, as I stood to check on the horses.

Of course, this was far more than that. I found Balder easily, his gray coat glimmering under the stars and moon far above. Moving as quickly and quietly as I could, I put his saddle on, tied down the loose gear and slid his bridle over his head. Batman snorted low and I put a hand to him. "You stay here."

A thought occurred to me. I'd done it before, sabotaging Maks's equipment so he was slowed. I took Batman's gear, moving swiftly, and hid it deeper in the courtyard garden, far from Batman. I patted his neck and kissed him on his nose. "Look after him for us, and go slow, old friend."

He gave a low snort and pushed at me with his

nose, wiggling it around and looking for treats in my pockets.

Lila clung to my shoulder as I strode away from the garden to the hidden doorway I'd found in the dreamscape. I opened the vine-covered wood door and let myself through, Lila right with me, clutching my shoulder. Mamitu waited for me on the other side.

"This way," she said softly, beckoning me forward with one hand, the other holding aloft a torch.

I followed her around the inner circle of the castle, her skirts swishing across the ground in front of us, stirring up dust. "Not many come this way, I guess?"

"No. None take my help. They have all believed I mean them harm or wish to stop them," she said as she stopped in front of an iron-hinged door. She paused and waved her hand over the solid lock. It opened with a groan, and an icy wind blew through the hallway.

Lila let out a low hiss. "It should not be blowing wind in here."

"Why don't they take your help?" I asked.

"Because until you, all have come to overthrow Asag; they have been men." She gave me a tired smile. "And what use have they of an old woman like me, and any knowledge I might give them to succeed?"

My eyebrows shot up. "If you're old, I'm the fucking Storm Queen."

She gave a low hiss. "Do not say that name here. She is not the legend that many want to believe of her."

Now that was news to me. "Seriously? I thought—"

"Another tale, for another time," she said. "For now, let us find you a weapon worthy of your cause."

The door swung inward, a puff of dust on the air as the lanterns about the room lit of their own volition, one at time until the room was as bright as if the midday sun shone through the roof. Then again, it could be all the silver, gold, and jewels the lights reflected off.

Weapons of all kinds lined the walls, lay on tables, some even stuffed in baskets as if the overflow had just been too much to properly display.

"Choose wisely," she said softly.

I shot a look to her. "That is what the knight said to Indiana Jones in the tale of the Last Crusade."

Mamitu just waved me ahead of her with one hand. "Again, I cannot help you here. Just know that there are some weapons far more dangerous than others."

"Can't be worse than the flail," Lila muttered.

I snorted and agreed, but then a slow chill rippled down my spine as if her words were a taunt. A dare.

I walked through the room but spoke to Mamitu. "You said you were cursed, like me. How are we the same?"

She stood by the open door. "You are cursed to live a life of adventure, cat. Have you not seen it in your waking hours? And I, I am cursed to try to change destiny when it does not want to be changed."

The weapons were a treasure trove of goodies. Bows and arrows, axes, and yes, even a flail, swords of all sorts, daggers, and spears. There was no rhyme or reason to much of them. Though I paused at the flail, I turned away. A real flail was far too heavy and unwieldy for me to manage from horseback.

*Here.*

I turned at the sound of the whisper in my head. "Sentient weapons?" I asked.

Mamitu shook her head. "There are weapons from all who have tried to battle their way to Asag over the two thousand years he has ruled. I know not what there is and what there isn't, with exception of a few legendary pieces." She stepped into the room and pointed at a massive broadsword against the wall. "Excalibur is here. As is the bow that shot Achilles. The twin blades of a Tracker." With each, she pointed but I didn't feel a draw to them.

*Here, beneath the floor.*

I stopped walking and looked down at the stone I stood on. Solid black where all the others were gray. Mamitu's breath hitched.

Crouching, I ran my fingers around the edge of the stone and easily pried it up. Inside the square was a single weapon, nothing all that fancy. A curved dagger of the desert, the blade the length of my arm. The handle was a smooth black wood that fit into my hand.

Mamitu cleared her throat. "That is the weapon you would take?"

I looked up at her, shocked that I even had a weapon in my hand. "I held the flail made by the Jinn masters and it tried to eat my soul on more than one occasion. This feels . . . similar. Why?"

Mamitu shook her head. "I only know that the man who held that blade died a horrible death, one that I will not even speak the details of."

"Is that why you put the weapon under the stone?" I asked, standing, blade in hand. Mamitu tensed and I lowered the tip of the weapon.

"I put it there because it spoke to me of death," she whispered. "I would not carry it for all the freedom in the world."

Lila flew off my shoulder and turned to face me. "And *that's* the blade you picked. Of course, it is. You know, you could at least try not to pick things that are nasty."

The blade's handle didn't heat in my hand and there were no more whispers in my head. I looked down into the hole in the floor to see a leather scabbard. I scooped it up and slid the blade into it. The scabbard went across my back and I tied it in place. "It will do."

Mamitu pressed her palms together and bowed over her fingertips. "Be careful, Zamira of the western deserts. I believe your fate is changing even now with the choice of that blade."

I froze where I was. "Lila?"

"Will survive even with this new choice," Mamitu whispered. "Your fate has become . . . murky."

Lila shook her head. "Nope, put it back." She flew behind me and pulled on the weapon, jerking me backward. "Put the knife back."

"She cannot. They have chosen one another," Mamitu said, a sigh falling from her lips. "Go, ride out now and do what you can to save your man."

Mamitu turned and left us there, standing in

the weapons room. "Lila, it will be okay. She said murky, not murdered," I said.

"Not funny," Lila snapped. "You are the only family I have. You'd better not die on me."

I held a hand out and she landed on my wrist as if she were a bird of prey and I her falconer.

She crawled up my arm to my shoulder. "Just . . . be careful with it, okay?"

I went to a table across the room and the pile of shotgun shells that lay there. Some were slugs, some were buckshot. I scooped up handfuls and shoved them into my bag on my hip. Next to the slugs was a pile of grenades. I turned one over to see if it would fit in my mini grenade launcher that sat under the barrels of my shotgun. They looked right, and they would be good to have on hand. I took the four.

"Did she say you could take more stuff?" Lila asked as I stuffed my bag as full as I dared.

"She said one weapon, nothing about ammo," I pointed out as I left the room and made my way through the curving castle to the courtyard.

Out in the open air, I studied the sky and where the crescent moon hung. We were barely past midnight. That would give me at least a six-hour lead on Maks.

I went to Balder; Mamitu stood next to him. "You are ready to go?"

"I can't fucking well go in the morning and not expect him to fight me on leaving him behind," I said, struggling to keep my words low and still angry as a cat dunked in a tub full of cold water. I wasn't angry at her, not really. I was angry that again I needed to part ways with the other half of my heart.

She smiled and slid a hand over Balder's face. He leaned into her touch and that gave me as much solace in trusting her as anything else. Balder was an amazing judge of character.

For example, he'd never liked my douche of an ex-husband, Steve. In fact, he'd kicked him in the balls once. At the time, I'd thought it was just an accident. Now I had no doubt it was on purpose. Just one more reason to love my mount.

Mamitu continued to love on Balder. "Then I give you one last warning, one last piece of advice. The path to the vessel is as dangerous as you can imagine. Travel only during the day. The rabisu will be waiting in the night for you, and though they look somewhat weak, they are anything but and should not be underestimated. Ignore their song, plug your ears if you must, do not invite them in and whatever you do, *do not let them bite you*." She handed me a small bag. "This is food and small supplies. It is all I can do without tipping my hand to Asag."

I took the bag and tied it to my waist. "Thank you." I looked her in the eyes. "If you want me to succeed, keep him here as long as you can. Tell him . . . tell him why I left without him. Beg him to stay here, for me and Lila. Or give him another task. Anything to delay him."

I grabbed a piece of paper from my bag and scribbled a note on it. "Here, put this somewhere he will find it. Please. It will help."

She pressed her fingers together. "Fate has brought you two together; you will find him again *if* he lives through this journey. Go north, that is the path you must take. You will find the signs that will lead you to the vessel."

*If.* I did not like that word, but it was better than *he's for sure dead.* I hopped up on Balder and Mamitu opened a side door in the stone wall that I would have sworn was not there before. But it didn't matter. I was out and it shut behind me, and all I could hope was that Maks would forgive me when he woke.

That he would be alive when this was all said and done.

The high walls of red stone rose above us as I turned Balder to the north. I let him pick his speed which was a full gallop as we raced away from the round castle, away from Mamitu and her ghouls, away from Maks and Batman.

Only then did I let the tears flow down my cheeks. I should have known we'd not be given an easy go of this, that we'd once more be forced to make hard choices. Lila tucked her head under my chin.

"He'll understand. He'd do the same were the positions reversed."

But I wasn't so sure. Maks and I had differing views on how to tackle problems. He always wanted a united front, and while I agreed with him for the most part, there were times you had to take action and do what you had to—even if it meant leaving someone you loved behind.

"I don't know," I said softly. "I want to believe he'll forgive me, but I'd be pissed if he left me." Then again, I was better at figuring out when he was up to something. He was an open book in many ways, easy to read with his emotions all but worn on his sleeves.

Lila snorted. "Then he shouldn't sleep so deeply."

I sighed and leaned into Balder as he navigated the moonlit valley of stones with ease. "You forgave me for leaving you behind, didn't you?" I asked my horse.

He gave a low whinny which could have been yes, could have been no. "I'm going to take that as a yes."

I blew out a final shaky breath and looked ahead. "I'll feel bad later. Let's get this damn Vessel of Vahab and get back to him as soon as we can."

The dark of the night seemed to tighten around us as we galloped away, and I knew without a shadow of a doubt that I was leaving a piece of my heart and soul behind.

"Please forgive me" was all I could whisper as we put miles between us and Maks.

## 9

MAKS

He rolled onto his side on the soft castle ground and reached for Zam, looking for her warmth and the solid sureness of her body close to his that gave him the strength to face the challenges that came their way. His fingers found only grass and the lips of Batman tickling away at him. He opened his eyes to the early morning light. Batman leaned over him and whuffled his nose into his hair and along his ears.

"Get out of here," Maks laughed and gently pushed his horse's face off his own. Batman was having none of it and continued to push his way into his space. "I'm up. I'm up, okay?"

He pushed to his feet and dusted a few bits of grass off his pants. For sleeping on the ground, he felt remarkably rested. He did a slow turn. "Where's Balder?"

Batman gave a low whinny and tossed his head.

"They have gone."

Maks spun to stare at Mamitu. "What?"

"The cat, the dragon, and the unicorn have gone."

Everything in him slowed to a halt, and for a moment, he feared his knees would buckle. "No, Zam wouldn't leave—"

"To save your life, would she leave?" Mamitu asked quietly. "To save hers, would you take another task?"

That froze him in place. "What are you saying?"

"This journey is not for you, Maks, Jinn master. The Vessel of Vahab contains something that would destroy you should you draw close to it. The reason your memories contain nothing of the east are within that vessel." She pressed her fingers together. "If you go after your mate and the dragon, all three will die."

He stared hard at her, seeing the truth, but also the deception in her face. "You lied to her. And you know what I am."

Her lips tightened. "No, I did not lie to her. But once she left, the lines of destiny changed, as they do with each choice made. If you want to help keep her and Lila safe, you will not follow her."

It took an effort for him to stand there and not snarl. "And what would you have me do?"

Mamitu smiled, but there was a tightness to it he didn't like. "You have connections still with the Jinn of the west."

He frowned. "Not really. They are all free of a master to rule them."

"I did not ask you if you could rule them, I asked if you have connections," she said.

Maks looked her over, not fully trusting her, but also not sure he could deny what she was saying. Everything in him said he needed to go after Zam and Lila. Even though he understood why they'd left the way they did.

"And if I go after Zam and Lila?" he asked quietly. "What then? What do you glimpse of our future?"

Her eyes clouded, the gold in them dimming. "If you choose to go after her now, you put her life in danger, as well as your own. It is why she left. It is why she asked me to beg you on her behalf to not follow. To let her do this with only her mount and the dragon."

His jaw ticked. The choice now was whether or not to trust this woman they barely knew. This goddess of fate and destiny who claimed that him being with Zam would hurt her. He put the heels of his hands to his eyeballs and for once wished that the other Jinn masters had not left him.

That he had someone to turn to for advice.

"She left without a weapon," he said finally, lowering his hands.

Mamitu shook her head. "No, I sent her with one that is forged with the blood of the damned and a sister weapon to the flail she once carried. It will serve her well and keep her safe. Now, will you do your part and go to your Jinn?"

"Why?"

"Because without them, I am not sure I can contain the Vessel of Vahab."

He stared hard at her. "What are you saying?"

She sighed. "Vahab is the first Jinn that the demon born of the fires of hell had cast into the desert to torment travelers and kin alike. He is your forebearer and the reason for the forbidding. It could never get out to the Jinn masters that there was a power waiting for them in the deserts of the east. A power that could be used."

He stared at her, not sure anything she could have said would have been worse. "Then why bring the Jinn here?"

"Because you will need all their strength to contain Vahab."

"He's in a vessel, isn't he? Why would that

change?" He found his voice getting louder and didn't care, but he could feel something coming that he didn't like, a danger that no one had told Zam about before she'd rushed off thinking to save him.

Mamitu's clasped hands turned white around the knuckles. "It is Asag's failsafe. Should someone be able to bring the Vessel of Vahab to me, it will open, and Vahab will be the next master of this domain, protecting Asag further and killing those who would try to ride through his territory."

Maks let his knees buckle then. "You knew, didn't you, when you had your ghouls attack us in the desert."

Mamitu knelt beside him. "No, I did not. But when I saw you riding in, I saw the pieces of a weapon that could free us all from Asag and keep your own desert safe in doing so."

A shaky breath slid out of him, one he couldn't believe was going to be followed with the words he spoke next. "I will gather what Jinn I can and bring them here." He paused. "But why can you release me now?"

"Only one group can see the vessel at a time. It allows me to bend the rules and send you away, unscathed," she said. "I am no killer, Maks. I am a seer. Asag has made me . . . no matter on that. He needs to be stopped."

Maks pushed once more to his feet. "You should have been honest with us."

"Zam would never have left you if she did not understand fully that you would die," Mamitu said, her eyes sad. "And now you must understand that all of our lives are not only in her hands, but yours as well."

Jaw clenched, he turned to Batman and looked to where the saddle had been last. A small smile twitched over his lips. "She hid my gear to slow me down."

It took him only a few minutes to find the saddle, bridle, bedroll and the rest of his pack. Stuffed into the pack was a single note.

*I love you, Maks, and I could not bear this world knowing I didn't do everything I could to keep you safe. Please forgive me. I will be back as soon as I can.*

He folded the note and tucked it in his shirt against his heart. "I love you too, you damn crazy cat."

After saddling Batman, he pulled himself astride and glanced at Mamitu who waited patiently for him. "How long?"

"Three weeks. You have three weeks before Zam and Lila are back by the path that fate has shown me for them."

Three weeks was going to cut it close, especially without any magic to help him along. "And when I bring the Jinn, Asag could steal their power too." That stopped him in his tracks. "How is that going to help take down Vahab?"

"I never said you were going to take him down," Mamitu said and tapped her fingers against his leg. "I said you were going to contain him."

Of all the people in the world she could have said that to, and have them fully understand the cost, he was the one. He'd been a host to Marsum's spirit, to the spirits of all the Jinn masters, and she was asking him and the other Jinn to host Vahab.

"How much control will he have?"

She shook her head. "I know not. Only that you must be here with as many Jinn as you can, he is too strong."

He blew out a breath. "I will be here. If you see Zam coming and I am not here, send your ghouls to slow her down."

Mamitu bowed at the waist. "I will do all I can to help you see this through, Jinn master."

He turned Batman and urged the horse into a gallop out the front gates of the castle and back the way he'd ridden with Zam the day before.

"Be safe, my love," he whispered, praying that the wind would take his love and words to her.

## 10

Balder easily galloped through the remainder of the night, straight north away from Mamitu and her castle, away from Maks. I left the reins loose and let him pick his speed as the ground hardened beneath his hooves. I didn't dare touch the reins as I struggled not to turn him around. My head knew what was best, to leave Maks where he was safe—I'd seen the visions as clearly as if I'd been standing there, watching Maks be run through, liquified, and bitten to death. Leaving him behind was the only way. I knew it and yet it still hurt, digging into me.

Making me doubt my own actions once more.

Lila dozed in the crook of my arm, her mouth open as she snored and then snorted herself awake. "Are we there yet?"

I forced a smile as I looked down at her. "No. But we need to slow and give Balder a break. Maybe you want to do some recon and check out what we've got ahead of us?"

With a jaw-cracking yawn, she slithered out of my arms as if she would fall off Balder's back, spreading her wings at the last second and swooping along the ground for a moment before rising above our heads.

I eased Balder to a walk and then slid off his back, stretching my own legs. His dappled gray coat was slick with sweat, but even though he was breathing hard, I could feel the urge in him to go again, the tremble of muscles ready to run. He loved to race, and without Batman slowing us down, we could cover ground like nobody's business.

I patted his neck. "Take a breather, buddy. There is no point being crazy. You know Maks. He's probably just waking up now. And if Mamitu does as she said she would, she'll slow him down. Even if he tried, he'll never catch us."

A twinge of worry rippled through me. He still might try. He still might think he should be with us even though his death was certain. Would the goddess show him the same vision I'd seen of his death?

Balder blew out a big breath and cracked a

yawn big enough that he could flip his tongue out at me. I looked away from his goofing off to take in the view around us. Mountains climbed to the right of us; those had to be the ones Mamitu had said she'd give us permission to cross once we completed this task of finding the Vessel of Vahab. A mountain full of rhuks.

In front of us to the north, there didn't seem to be much of anything I would call memorable. More sand, more rocks, some rolling hills and ... I squinted, not sure if what I was seeing was what I was seeing.

For just a moment, I thought I was looking at a lion from my pride. I thought for a moment it was Ford.

Black fur rippled in the sun as the big cat loped toward us, and it was only when it was closer that I could see the size was off. I wanted to reach for a weapon. I wanted my flail, but it wasn't there.

I reached for the sword strapped to my back but didn't quite touch the handle. Just in case.

I stayed at Balder's side, halting him. Lila swept back to us. "Big cat coming. Looks like a jungle cat. Like you when you're big."

Jungle cat. That was my other shape. This could go either way.

Words rippled through my mind.

*I am sister to the flail.*

"Sister to the flail, huh?" I reached back and pulled the short sword from its scabbard across my back. The weight of it was easy in my hand, and there was no locking onto my palm like the flail had done. That wasn't what had my attention.

No, I was listening to the whisper of words through my head as the weapon settled against my palm. The sound of a woman crooning to her lover.

*Kill it, cut it to pieces, spill the blood, open the belly . . .*

I grimaced and squeezed the handle a little harder. "Shut your trap."

*Kill, kill, kill, kill . . .* the refrain was soft, like a lullaby of the most deadly sort. Worse was the urge that came with it to do as it suggested, to lop the head off the cat in front of me without waiting to see if it was even dangerous. And just like that, I shoved the blade back into its scabbard.

"Fuck. This thing was a terrible idea," I whispered. Lila looked at me, her eyes full of concern.

"The sword?"

I gave her a tight nod, then locked my eyes on the shifter headed toward us. Sure, it was a possibility that it wasn't a shifter, just your average jungle cat wandering through a desert, but I was inclined to doubt it.

The big cat slowed to a jog, and then to a walk.

Tongue hanging out, it didn't seem interested in attacking us.

"Can you speak?" I asked.

The head bobbed once. "Water. Please."

I grabbed my waterskin off the front of the saddle with a quick movement and tossed it at the cat. He shifted to two legs, as quickly as I could, still fully dressed unlike other shifters, and crouched over the waterskin. He pulled the cork and took a few quick swallows, then paused, his eyes closed as he let the water settle.

Smart, he'd been in the desert long enough to know not to guzzle the water. "What are you doing out here?" I asked. "Aren't these Mamitu's lands?"

He grimaced. "They are. We are allowed to live here, just not allowed to cross out of the territory. East and west are forbidden, north and south are not."

Lila peered at him. "What are you doing out here with no food, no water, nothing?"

He sighed, took another swig of water and then tossed the empty skin back to me. I had another so I was not worried. "Just because Mamitu holds these lands doesn't make them safe. I've been hunting rabisu."

I glanced at Lila. "Mamitu warned us of them. How bad are they?"

He rubbed the back of his hand against his

mouth. "They killed my family, my wife and children. I'd destroy them all if I could. Filth of the earth and nothing but ravenous spirits given physical form." He spit to the side which in the desert was a big thing. You give up moisture for nothing but the most important things in life.

I pointed in the direction we had to go. "Let me guess, up there to the north, that's where these rabisu are?"

"It's where they breed, yes. There are caverns full of them. But they hunt in the jungle." He nodded, grimaced, and his eyes rolled back in his head as he went to the ground. Lila shot forward first.

Her wings fluttered as she danced around him. "I think he has bites on him. Here on his chest."

I grabbed my pack and the hacka paste tucked away. It was the only healing ointment I had, so we were about to find out what it did against a rabisu bite.

"Don't hurt my daughter, please," he whimpered through a convulsion.

The pain in his voice tugged at me. His dark skin was far too pale, his body twitching and dancing against whatever it was he saw in his mind's eye.

"Lila, sit at his head. If you control him there,

he won't thrash as much. 'Cause this is going to hurt like a bitch."

She did as I said and clutched at his ears. "I don't think I can pin him down well."

I spun open the jar of hacka paste, the thick red glittering stuff sticking fast to my fingers. I spread it over the two bites on his chest and he groaned. Lila crooned to him, singing something or other and he stilled, his head tipping toward her.

Next came the really fun part. I grabbed a match, struck it with my fingernail and lit the hacka paste on fire.

The shifter screamed, his body arching upward, teeth and fangs flashing as Lila held his head and I tried to hold him at the waist. I grabbed a handful of my cloak and shoved it in his mouth to muffle the sound. He bit down, just missing my fingers and I snatched my hand back.

We did not need the sounds of his pain to bring down some goddess-forsaken monstrosity on us.

His scream turned into a low mutter and he slumped flat on his back with a big exhalation.

Lila looked at me. "Is he dead?"

I shook my head. "Passed out. Let's get him on Balder. He's going to have to come with us for now, we can't leave him here. He'll die for sure."

Grabbing hold of his hands, I settled him up

onto my shoulder and stumbled only a little under his weight. Balder went down to one knee for me and I slid the man over his back. "Buck him off hard if you think he's waking up, okay? I don't want you hurt."

Balder gave a single bob of his head.

Lila flitted around and finally landed on the front of the saddle. "You think this is supposed to be the love of my life?"

I stared hard at her. "Honestly?"

"Yes, tell me honestly."

"No, Lila. I don't think the love of your life is going to be a half-dead shifter whose just lost his wife and children." But even as I said it, I saw her wings slump, and I took a slow breath before I asked the question I couldn't quite believe I was asking. "You think he is?"

She frowned and her purple eyes darkened. "I don't know, there was just a moment there when I was holding his head . . . I think I'm just hoping. She gave me hope, you know that's the worst thing sometimes."

I shrugged. "Not the worst thing, but a hope can be destructive for sure if you let it take you onto any path that presents itself."

She settled herself as close to the stranger as she could. "Well, to be sure, I'll let myself like him a little. Then we can see."

I blinked a few times, opened my mouth, thought better of it and started walking. "What did you see up there ahead of us?"

"Just more of the same. The other side of this hill is a long sloping valley that runs north for a good amount of time. And it's more jungle than desert so there should be plenty of hunting, plenty of cover from the heat. But I'm assuming that's the jungle he was talking about the rabisu hunting in. To either side of it are sheer cliff faces that rise hundreds of feet."

She was probably right, about the jungle being the one that the shifter was talking about, and there would be plenty of hiding spots too for the rabisu that had apparently taken their share of bites out of our new friend. I wanted to ask him all the questions bubbling under my skin, but he was out cold and hadn't so much as twitched in the last half-hour that we'd been walking.

We reached the top of the next hill, and as I looked down into the valley, I could see how very right Lila had been. The jungle was spread out ahead of us, only about three miles wide in the center of the valley, but as far north as I could see and then some. To either side were the cliffs that rose with no way to get Balder over them. Here and there were openings into the cliffs.

Hollowed-out dens for the rabisu. I wrinkled my nose.

"Can't go over it, can't go under it, can't go around it," I whispered. "Gotta go through it."

Lila flew ahead of me. "Yeah. I don't like that we're being funneled. You do that with things you want to eat."

I blew out a sharp breath. "Really, did you have to say it out loud?"

She back-winged so she could hover just in front of my face. "You didn't think it?"

"Of course, I thought it!" I threw one hand up. "I just didn't want to point out that we're being treated like cattle sent to the slaughter."

She dropped to the ground and trotted beside me, not something she did often. "Might as well walk with the rest of you moos."

I took a mock swing at her with my boot and she scooted forward, laughing as she flipped herself into the air. Her eyes widened as she stared at something behind us, and her laughter died off.

"Oh, please don't tell me my luck has shown up to the party," I said, forcing myself to turn and look at what had spooked her. It took me only a moment to register that we were looking at something new to us, something dangerous.

Something we really needed to avoid if I were going to guess at the creatures' intentions.

Two rather large individuals stood at the top of the hill we'd just crested and were looking down at us. Their skin was light gray and pebbled as though they were stuck together with small stones and cement. They had four arms each, with big flat feet that were split into only two toes that gripped the ground like fat talons.

Just like the tracks from the Blackened Market.

Their heads were jammed directly onto their shoulders, with no necks that I could see. When they looked around with eyes that were too small and almost indistinguishable in color, their entire heads swiveled, kind of like an owl's did.

In the middle of their chests a symbol was tattooed, or maybe engraved was a better word. The image was that of a crescent moon on fire.

Worse than all that?

The pair hunched forward and revealed their back muscles and the wings attached to them and flexed them wide, showing off the thick leather hide.

Freaking wings.

"Lila, they can fly. That's not good."

"Yeah, I'd concur with that. Maybe they aren't going to bother us?"

The two beasties locked onto us. One pointed, and the two of them roared as they leapt into the air, shattering the stillness.

Lila eeped. "Nope, I was wrong."

I leapt up onto Balder's back and put my heels to him. The injured shifter in front of me was going to get bruises along his belly from being bounced along, but it was that or probably a real shitty death at the hands of our new friends. I hoped he appreciated the efforts we were going to in order to keep him alive.

Balder took off down the hill and I leaned back, one hand on the shifter's belt to keep him in place, the other hand straight out behind me for balance as we galloped down the slope. Lila clung to my chest, staring at our tail.

"Lila, what are they doing?" I yelled.

Her answer was less than comforting. "Don't ask, go faster!"

I dared a look back and wished I hadn't. They were running, using their wings and the downhill pull of gravity to move fast enough that they were closing in on us.

They were closing in on Balder, who was quite literally faster than any horse out there.

Sweet baby Jesus on a crippled donkey, I did not feel like fighting those monstrosities. The thought of grabbing hold of the short sword again was enough to make my stomach tighten in a terrible way.

If I didn't have to pick it up ever again, I would

die happy. Strike that, I didn't need to think about dying right then.

The thing was when you were the smallest creature in the desert, you learned quickly to distinguish the fights you could win, and the ones to run from. This was not a fight that would come out well, if my guess was spot on.

We were less than a minute away from the jungle, but I wasn't sure we'd lose these beasties. "Lila, we're going to have to fight, or at least try to slow them down."

She shot ahead of me to the bottom of the slope and turned to face the oncoming creatures, her face twisted up in a snarl that if she'd been able to shift into her larger form would have been as terrifying as the creatures behind us. As it was, she just looked kind of fierce, like a kitten being tough.

A moment later Balder hit the flat of the valley bottom and I spun him around and jumped off his back, pulling the sword from my back.

*Destroy, kill, maim, gut their bellies . . .*

The handle didn't warm, though part of me wished it did. I'd take the handle heating over the words being whispered through my skull any day.

The creature in the lead had its wings outstretched and pumping hard to pick up speed. Four sets of hands reached for me, the tips of those hands not curved claws, but dagger-like points.

"Knife hands!" I yelled both in horror and warning as I ducked under the first swing of the heavy, dagger hands. I went flat to the ground and rolled to my back as the creature swept over me, moving too fast to stop itself.

With a grunt I swung the sword one-handed, clipping the beast across the ass, chipping away stone. There was no blood, no flesh tearing.

There was no cry of pain from the monster.

Mind you, I did have its attention now. It spun and opened its mouth which was really just an open dark hole without any teeth. And it bellowed at me like a rutting bull, the sound echoing across the valley.

"Zam, I'm dodging the other one easily, but it's not slowing!" Lila shouted.

"Acid?" I asked as I bounded onto my feet, holding the sword with a hand. It wasn't as light as the flail, but I could manage one-handed.

"I don't have a lot. I used most on the ghouls!"
*Let me kill them.*

"Yeah, yeah, give me a minute!" I snapped. The creature turned and took a step toward Balder trotting away, balancing the shifter on his back. I picked up a rock and threw it at the beast to make sure all its attention was on me and not Balder and the unconscious shifter. "Balder, get to the jungle, go!"

The rock hit the chest of the creature right over the crescent moon and fire, and . . . absorbed right into it. "Oh, that's not good." I grimaced. "Lila, they're literally made of rock!" I'd kind of been hoping it was just a look and a style of rough hide and armor.

She yelped and I glanced as she didn't fully dodge the points of the other rock creature's hands, the tips raking down her side.

If I'd had the flail, at least I would've been able to suck the life out of these bastards. I stepped toward the rock creature in front of me, gripped the sword hard as it giggled death in my head, and took a swing, changing my trajectory at the last second into a thrust.

I drove the sword right into the center of the creature's chest and yanked it upward. The sword screeched like a fucking banshee as it cut through the stone, the metal on rock screaming into the air.

The rock head seemed to pause, though, and consider what was happening to it. The eyes lit up, the color changing from nothing to . . . bright orange.

*Kill it faster, kill it harder,* the sword whispered. *Hurry, before he sees you!*

"Who are you?" The rock monster stared at

me, its voice not the deep baritone of the bellow, but a higher pitched tenor. The head twisted to the left and the right and I yanked the sword to keep his, its, their, eyes on me and not Lila or Balder.

I stared into the eyes, feeling them weigh me, seeing them judge me as unworthy.

"I'm your worst fucking nightmare," I growled as I leaned into the sword, driving it into the chest, all the way to the hilt despite the screeching of the metal on stone. With a snarl, I jerked the sword upward, straight through where a neck should have been, and through the head, bisecting the orange eyes.

A bellow from behind me sent a chill through my sweat-soaked body.

A third rock head was joining us.

The orange eyes began to fade. "Interesting. I could use you."

And then the color was gone as was the voice.

But the urge for me to go on a slaughtering rampage was overwhelming me, driving me to be stupid, and I didn't do stupid.

Desert born as I was, I knew one thing for sure. Stupid got you killed more often than not.

What I did know was simple. These creatures weren't really alive, which meant they wouldn't tire, and killing them was harder than anything else I'd faced in a long while. "Lila, any luck with the acid?"

"It didn't work!" she hollered back, confirming what I already suspected.

We were outmatched with these creatures, which meant it was time to go.

I took a step and shifted to four legs, taking on my house cat form. I shot forward between the legs of the rock creature that was slowly going to its knees and bolted toward the jungle. Not before the rock head reached for me, the tip of one of its dagger-pointed fingers slicing across my back, opening the flesh. I bit back a yowl as warm blood trickled down my back legs.

It felt as though fire burned across my body and I had to fight the urge to stop and roll, as if I were indeed on fire. Lila was right with me as we plunged into the undergrowth of the jungle. The sounds behind us told me the rock creatures had not given up.

I scented the air and steered us away from where Balder had gone. We could find him later, but not if he was cut into pieces. Our best bet was to pull the monstrosities in a different direction. To hide and hope they looked past us.

Madness, this was madness.

So much for being excited to start a new journey into an adventure. I grimaced and dove under a section of thick green fronds. Lila shot down with me, breathing hard. Her scales glittered with her blood too and her muscles twitched as hard as my own were flinching and jumping.

The shaking in my own limbs was tough to keep under control, like I was no longer in charge of my own body. "Poison fingertips," I whispered.

And promptly passed out.

I floated in and out of consciousness on the floor of the jungle, Lila next to me doing the same while the rock heads thundered about looking for us. They wouldn't get tired, they wouldn't stop. Which meant we were in serious trouble. And I couldn't fucking well so much as twitch my tail on my own, never mind run.

Hallucinations ripped through me as the world spun, the heat of the poison under my skin burning me from the inside out. Visions of death, of the sword in my hand, of Maks falling under my hand . . . his blue eyes begging me not to kill him, of Lila screaming my name.

Of the sword in my hand laughing.

I drunkenly curled up around Lila, the only solid in the moments of delusion where I saw

Maks and was sure he was there, calling for us. I wanted to yell to him, to tell him we were there but I didn't dare. The rock heads would find us and they'd find him. I didn't leave him behind only to have him die because I was hallucinating.

Beside me, Lila mumbled and I put a paw over her face like a drunk friend trying to help her other drunk friend shut up while the cops searched the bushes for them. She quieted and the heavy footsteps faded. The sound of birds filled the air again and, miracle of miracles, the rock heads were gone. I thought.

The light in the jungle had shifted, changing from early morning to very late afternoon—hours had slid by. My mouth was dry and fuzzy, and I didn't like the way my head felt, but at least I was awake. Awake and alive. The poison was still there, still eating away at me, but I was no longer in the heat of it.

"Maks wouldn't have survived this," Lila whispered and then groaned. "Even if he'd been able to shift to his caracal form, which I don't know that he could, he wouldn't have been small enough. That's what saved us."

She wasn't wrong, and I made a mental note to point this out to him when I saw him next.

Being small had saved us.

Wobbling, I stepped out from around the thick

leaves and slowly followed my nose to Balder. Lila's belief that Maks would have died didn't quite hold up if Balder was okay. That thought propelled me forward faster until I was running as quickly as I could, wobbling on every other step, following the scent of my horse.

He'd gone deep into the jungle, far deeper than I would have thought. A mile ticked by, and then another. "Balder!" I shifted to two legs, stumbled and ended up clinging to a tree, sliding partway down it, the bark biting into my hands.

Nope, that was ants. I flicked my hands, knocking the biting ants off and started forward again. A soft whinny called to me and I turned to the left. Balder lay on the ground against one wall of the valley, him and his still passed-out passenger hidden under a series of oversized fronds.

Blood spots splattered his dappled coat and I hurriedly knocked the biting ants off him. They'd been biting him, and he hadn't moved. "You are a good boy. The very best boy," I said as I cleared him of the bugs. He'd not moved even though he'd been bitten terribly. I took his reins and led him out from under the foliage, away from the bugs. Lila stumbled up to me and I scooped her up and set her on the back of the shifter, who finally stirred.

"We need to keep going," I said. "I don't think we should stop now."

"Agreed," Lila said. "My head feels like it's stuffed with cotton and sand."

I nodded and wished I hadn't. "Worse than a țuică hangover." I paused and dredged up an old quote. "Why, Lila, for my part, I say the poison has tampered with all five senses."

She groaned. "That's terrible. Not even the best quote from *The Merry Wives of Windsor*."

I would have smiled but every muscle in me was protesting. Protesting and then some. "Balder, can you lead?" I clung to the side of the saddle without even the strength to pull myself onto his back.

He did as I asked, stepping out and picking his way through the jungle. There were paths that he followed that could barely be seen, but they were enough to allow us easy passage. Or easier than if we'd had to bushwhack our way through.

We made it another mile by my calculations before I couldn't take another step. Hell, maybe it was ten miles. It surely felt like it was that long. "Enough. We have to stop."

I managed to push the shifter off Balder's back, and he hit the ground with a heavy thud. My apology was mumbled but it was the best I could do.

Shifters bounced well. I wasn't worried about him being hurt. Balder stood quietly as I hung from his side a moment longer then slowly slid to the ground.

"Lila?"

"Here." She thumped onto the ground next to me and rolled onto her back. "Their nails are terrible. Dirty. Filthy. Terrible."

I drew a breath, gagged and lay on my side. "The poison. I don't know how long . . . how long it will last."

She gagged and heaved next to me but didn't throw up, nor did she bring up any acid. Balder lay next to me and rolled, pushing my bag into my hands. I fumbled with the buckle and pulled out the hacka paste and smeared the last bit of it on Lila.

My fingers shook and I nearly dropped the lit match, but I managed to catch the paste on fire and she hissed as it sizzled, searing the healing paste and drawing out the poison from the scratches even while it healed them.

Lila grabbed at my hand that still had a little paste on it and froze. "I really hope he's a good guy, 'cause we are at his mercy."

I didn't look up as hands flipped me over to my belly and the back of my shirt was lifted. Fingers spread the dredges of the hacka paste onto my back and the heat was immediate, the paste thick and sticking into the wound edges.

There was the smell of sulfur, and I gritted my teeth against what was going to come as the match touched the paste. If the heat was intense before, it was nothing to the literal flames that raced across my skin. I hissed and growled under my breath as the flares slowly burned down and the hacka paste melted, puddling along my spine.

Lila stared past me. "You got a name, shifter?"

He drew a slow breath. "Jasten Wilson."

Now, there were very few things that could surprise me anymore in this world. One would be that a black leopard shifter like me was out there. Another would be that he had the same last name as me. Because my father had been a lion shifter. My mother carried the black jungle cat shape.

"Wilson." I rolled over. "Who was your father?"

He stared down at me and I could see the similarities there, just hints of my—our—father's face hardened from years of tough living. Dark hair like mine, and pale amber eyes, though his skin was several shades of a deeper brown than my own. He stared down at me and frowned. "You look familiar."

"You look like her brother," Lila blurted.

I rolled to a crouch, wobbled and then sat back

on my butt. "Well, that's a pretty big jump, and it's not for certain just because—"

"Just look at him!" Lila said. "And he has the same last name as you and who the hell uses last names here anyway? You do. You, and that's all I know and now him." She was freaking out, her wings twitching as she stumbled around my knees.

Her eyes were wide and she seemed more upset by this possibility than either Jasten or myself. "You an asshole?" I asked. I mean, let's be honest, my family wasn't known for being kind, never mind sane.

He frowned and sat back on his butt across from me. "Sometimes. I try not to be." He paused. "I don't understand how we can be siblings, though. My father died a long time ago, and you don't look old enough to fit the time period."

I yawned and leaned back against Balder, my eyes drifting shut. The poison was gone, but my body felt like I'd been pulled through a knothole backward. Repeatedly. "We probably aren't related then. My family tree is full of assholes."

He grunted. "Why is the little dragon freaking out then?"

I opened one eye to see that Lila was indeed pacing. I reached for her, grabbed her by the tail and pulled her into my arms. She squawked but then settled down quickly. "I'm not sure and she won't tell me until she's ready."

Jasten held a hand out, palm up. "Thank you. For saving me."

I put my hand in his, felt the solid warmth in him that was more than just skin, but an understanding that we'd saved each other. "Thanks for returning the favor."

He grinned, one side of his lips lifting more than the other. "You would have survived the poison. The pillars' poison is bad, but it's meant to just keep you still long enough for them to take you away, not kill you."

I pulled my hand from his and shook my head. "Pillars? That's what you call the rock things?"

Jasten leaned against a tree. "The pillar army. Belonging to none other than Asag, Gallu Demon, and sometimes known as the Beast from the East."

Lila shivered and I watched as our new friend touched her back gently. "Easy, little one. He can't find us here. The rabisu hold this area and the pillars are not allowed to come through other than at the fringes."

Lila looked up at him. "The rabisu are worse than the pillars?"

Jasten sighed. "I wouldn't say that. The rabisu can be killed, the pillars . . . they can be broken apart, but they can't be killed. They aren't really alive."

"That's what I was worried about," I said. "But they can be slowed down."

He shook his head. "No, I don't think so."

I leaned back, the hilt of the sword touching my shoulder and a whisper rolled through me.

*Kill him quick before he turns on you. He is not your brother. He has stolen your father's name.*

My jaw ticked and I pushed the whispers of the weapon away. Damn it, I should have picked anything else but this sword from Mamitu's weapons stash. A freaking fork would have been a safer choice.

Mind you, a fork wouldn't have sliced that pillar in half.

"Look, I think we should rest and then . . ." I trailed off and looked at Jasten. "You should go whatever way you're going."

He tipped his head to one side. "We aren't far into the jungle. The rabisu don't hunt out this way until the crescent moon fills."

I stared hard at him. "What do you mean? They have a pattern?"

He nodded once. "I don't know all of it, but, yes, there is a pattern. This outer edge of the valley is their least favorite hunting ground. All the small animals in the world and nothing larger to chew on."

Lila shivered. "So they don't attack smaller creatures?"

He leaned over and offered her his palm. She hopped into his hand and he set her on his bent knee. "You are safer than the rest of us. They don't like expending energy on a meal that isn't worth the chase. While they aren't thinkers, they aren't stupid either. Think of them as the ultimate predator. Their biggest draw is that they are like the ants —thousands of them at once is more than any one person can bear."

I closed my eyes. "Well, that's comforting."

We shared a quick meal pulled from my bags of dried jerky, piss-warm water, and a few big gulps of air. That was going to have to do until we could hunt up something more. All three of us needed the calories to heal the wounds from the rabisu and the pillars.

Balder snorted as I settled against his leg and I reached up and patted his belly. "Balder, you take first watch."

There was nothing left in me. I was exhausted. I needed sleep, and I needed to think about what to do next.

Despite the very obvious lack of safety where we were, sleep tumbled over me and I was out like a light as the sun set and the jungle dimmed around us.

I didn't move the entire time I was out, which meant when I did wake sometime in the dead of night, every muscle I had was stiff and my butt bones hurt. I lurched to my hands and knees and took in a deep breath, the distinct tang of coppery coins on the air.

Old blood was not something a shifter forgot the smell of—ever.

I stayed where I was, breathing it in. Trying to pinpoint where it came from.

To the left of us, something was in the bushes watching us, the smell of it almost imperceptible if the wind had been moving in a different direction. I kept my head still and just breathed the air in, tasting it across my tongue. Yeah, that was blood, old dried blood.

"Jasten." I whispered his name and he opened his eyes to look straight at me, the gleam of them in the night a perfect green glimmer despite the amber they were in the day. "Company."

"Rabisu," he said. "Two. One to the left of you. One behind me. Go for the head, take it off."

I didn't nod, just fluttered my eyelids in a quick blink, yes.

The leaves behind Jasten parted and a long set of fingers stretched out toward him. When I say long, they were easily a foot in length, and looked more like spider legs with additional joints. I stared hard at the pale fingers and finally the large flat palms, wondering just who the hell this place had pissed off to get so many uglies living in one stretch of land.

As the fingers dropped to Jasten's shoulder, I felt the touch on my own shoulder on the left of me.

A moment passed, the air stilled and the fingers tightened hard. I spun on my knees, dragging the rabisu with me, reached up and grabbed it by the wrists and snapped it forward onto the ground.

There was a sharp crack of bones and a head rolled toward us. The face of the other rabisu was frozen in death with a wide open O of a mouth and two overlong fangs hanging from the upper jaw. Like a snake. Eyes that were wide and milky, sightless now. But were they sightless before?

"Ugly fucker, aren't you?" I wrapped my hands around the rabisu's throat, and it launched at me, all claws and open mouth. I rolled with it across the ground as I scrabbled for the short blade I kept in the top of my boot.

"Fucking kill it!" Jasten snarled as he put a boot onto the creature's head, pinning it. I yanked my blade and slit the rabisu's throat through to the spine. It flopped and bopped like a chicken with its head cut off.

"The fresh blood will call to more of them. We have to go." Jasten stood, and he wobbled almost as much as I did. Only he was aiming to leave the jungle the way we'd just come in, facing the south end.

Course, he hadn't seen the rock heads we'd dealt with even if he had helped us with the wounds and poison.

"You can't go that way," Lila said. "Rock monsters."

He jerked to a halt and twisted around to look at her. "They won't be there now."

She bobbed her head once and flew to rest on Balder's rump. "We have to go through the jungle. Well, at least, we do. You can go wherever you like."

He looked at me and I nodded, already seeing our paths diverging. "Any more you can tell us about these rabisu? Seeing as we are obviously going into their territory?"

Jasten put a hand on the tree closest to him, balancing himself. "Take them out at the head if you can. They have terrible vision but excellent hearing and sense of smell, and maybe extrasensory that guides them. If there are two, there are more. They typically hunt in pods."

"How big is a pod?" Lila whispered.

"Twelve to fifteen on average," he said. "They leave smaller animals alone and take down only the big ones, like I said earlier. Lila will be the safest of you three."

I shot a look at Lila. "What about Balder? He can't be hidden."

She bit her bottom lip. "Then he has to go. We can't risk him."

Balder shook his head and stomped a foot. I touched his neck. "Just like Maks, if it means we can do this without getting you killed, I'm going to do it."

I blew out a breath and looked at Jasten. "I need to ask you to do something, and understand, I don't ask lightly."

Jasten bowed at the waist. "For saving my life, I will do what I can."

One last breath and I handed him Balder's reins. "Take my horse with you."

## 12

---

MAKS

Riding Batman to the west of Mamitu's castle, it didn't take Maks long to decide that this was a stupid idea, listening to a person who was for all intents and purposes a stranger. It took all of about fifteen minutes to pass before he turned Batman and booted him toward the east.

Maybe Mamitu would try to stop him, but she'd said the choice was his as to where he would go. He wasn't sure, but as he rode past her castle heading straight east, he saw her at the top. She held up one hand in a long farewell, but other than that there was nothing. No shifting of perspective, nor was he suddenly seeing himself riding in another direction.

She let him go.

Even though they both knew the weapon Zam had would want to strike him down. Made for killing Jinn, among other things.

He grimaced. Of all the things Zam could have chosen, why did it have to be *that* weapon?

The thing was, she'd fought off the flail as it tried to take her life, and she'd made it work for her instead of against her. He believed in her enough that he would risk his life to be by her side. She would never hurt him. He just didn't believe it.

Zam, Lila, and Balder would be a long ways ahead of him. He and Batman would have to ride hard and all day if they were going to have even a chance at catching up to them, but he was going to try.

Batman gave a deep blowing grunt as he galloped along. "I know," Maks said. "I know. But the thing is, what if me being with her actually keeps her alive? What if me being with her is what keeps the sword from doing her in? We don't know this Mamitu from any other supernatural out there. She could be fooling us all. She could be just like Merlin or Ishtar for all we know."

Another snort from Batman as he slowed, unable to sustain the harder pace as he once had, and then he gave his head a shake, flipping his mane side to side.

Maks eased back in his saddle. "I don't know that I'm right. I just know that Zam and I are strongest when we are together. And I can't let her go into this battle alone. This is not her burden to bear alone. I agreed to help the hatchlings too. I swore it."

Batman let out a fart and Maks grimaced. "Don't shit on my thoughts, horse. I'd rather be with her and know that I've done everything I can to keep her safe, and to keep my promise. And if she's going to be difficult about it and try to kill me, then and only then, I'll hogtie her."

They rode through the day heading straight east until the sun began to slide toward the horizon behind them. Maks twisted around in his saddle to get a view of the area. There was nowhere to settle for the night, just the open desert which had turned to rockier ground.

"No fire, my friend," he said as he loosened the saddle and took Batman's bridle off so he could nibble at the bits of tough desert grass that made a valiant effort at survival. From his bag, he pulled a few oat balls and rolled them across to Batman who followed his nose and scooped them up with nimble lips.

Maks ate some of the dried food he had and washed it down with lukewarm water. There would be no real rest for him, so rather than try to sleep, he sat cross-legged, eyes closed, to see if he could trace his magic.

"The thing about Jinn," he said softly to Batman, "is their power comes from the desert and from the first Jinn. Even a demon shouldn't be able to just cut me off like it was nothing. There has to be a hint, something in me that is still there. Maybe something of the masters that is left over in their memories."

His meditation deepened, and he floated within it, looking through memories that were not his own until they flowed around him and he could almost see his father, Marsum, sitting across from him.

"Pup, what in the hell are you doing out here in the eastern desert?" Marsum's voice echoed weirdly in his head, shocking the shit out of him. Maks startled and lost the thread of concentration, but quickly put himself back into a meditative state, finding that balance again.

"No one said *not* to come here, and how the hell are you even doing this? You went into the lava pit with the flail," Maks said. In his head, he could again see his father sitting across from him on the desert ground, though he had a feeling that if he opened his eyes, he'd lose the whole moment.

"Gods of the desert storm and sky, this is beyond

stupid. First of all, there is no real death in our world. There are always ways to come back—especially if your progeny needs you. You just have to know the paths. Second, let me guess, you decided to look for the hatchlings?" Marsum arched a brow at him.

Maks nodded. "Yes. But why does that surprise you?"

"It doesn't. You need to know a few things, though, if you're going to survive this place. I came here once as a young man, and my power was stolen from me. I had to go all the way to Asag to get them back. And I had to help him bind Mamitu as the price to get my power back."

Maks's mouth dropped open. "Wait, you made it all the way to him? And you're the reason Mamitu is stuck where she is?"

"I did, though I shouldn't have. I broke all the rules and that was why I made it, and if Mamitu figures out who you are, she'll kill you for sure. Zam will follow the rules where she can, and you never broke the rules, which means that you will both die if I don't help you. This place is not meant to be survivable to outsiders. The entire side of this desert is a trap, you young fool."

"I'm breaking the rules now," Maks said. "Mamitu wanted me to bring the Jinn to her."

There was a moment of pause where he wasn't

sure if Marsum would speak to him again. "Please tell me you weren't that damn stupid."

Maks sighed. "For a moment. I changed my mind." He paused. "She wants the Jinn to punish you, doesn't she?"

Marsum nodded. "That would be my guess. She's likely looking to see who has a connection to me. Again, I'd keep that quiet if I were you. Seeing as how that connection *is* you."

He let out a frustrated sigh and ran a hand over his head. "Okay, so what do you suggest then, knowing what you know about this place? Zam has the sister weapon to the flail."

Marsum was quiet for more than a moment this time, for long enough that Maks wasn't sure he was going to answer. "Lilith. You're telling me she has *Lilith*?"

Maks's heart beat a little harder. "Explain. Because the way you're saying that name makes me think this is even worse than I originally thought."

Marsum growled, stood and paced in front of Maks. Though it was all in his mind's eye, it was as real to Maks as if it were happening.

"Lilith is a demon, Maks. She was caught and condemned, her soul bound into that weapon. Her one purpose was to create more demons, but to also kill children. The irony is not lost on me that

Zam took that weapon to save the children of the dragons." Marsum paced. "But Zam has shown a remarkable ability to not be swayed by the power of a weapon created for destruction."

"Will it hurt her?"

There was another pause, Marsum thinking before he spoke, which was a remarkable thing to Maks. "Yes, it could. But perhaps there is a reason she had to take that weapon, I don't know. What I know is that it was the first Jinn who stuffed Lilith into the steel—he was the one to stop her rampage. Which is why any Jinn near it would be . . . in danger."

Rubbing his hands over his face, Maks let himself process what his father was saying. "This is . . . fuck, this is terrible."

"Oh, that's an understatement. If Zam holds the weapon long enough . . . the demon could possess her. You know, just to make it interesting. Wherever that cat goes, trouble follows, and Lilith will feed on that as surely as a beast feeding on a carcass." Marsum let out a dry laugh. "How am I not surprised Zam did this? I'm not, truly I'm not. And yet, I'm still shocked."

Maks found it hard to breathe around all this information that only compounded what Mamitu had told him. "What do I do? What about the fact that Zam has Jinn in her? Won't the weapon realize that?"

At that, Marsum was silent and when Maks looked up, he was gone.

So much for getting more help out of the old man.

Maks lay on his back and stared into the clear night sky, the stars shining brilliantly. "This is a mess."

Batman nuzzled the ground beside him and blew a stream of hot breath over Maks's face. He patted the horse as his thoughts rumbled around his head. The only thing he could do was keep moving forward, to the east.

To the east and hope he could catch Zam before she got in too much trouble.

L ila and I crouched under the heavy fronds of a palm tree on a branch three feet above the heads of a trio of rabisu skulking across the jungle ground below us.

I turned my head so she could see my mouth and read my lips. "*I'll beat thee, but I would infect my hands.*"

She pursed her lips and frowned. It took her almost a minute to mouth back, "*Timon of Athens?*"

I nodded and then it was her turn. Figuring out the insults by reading lips was much harder. But there was nothing else to do while the night waned and the rabisu hunted. They were not the terrors that everyone had made them out to be.

They were creepy as fuck, and moved in a stilted, freeze frame sort of way that made my heart clench in fear of what inhumanity they possessed. But otherwise, if you watched them long enough, they just looked . . . creepy. Weird. And they scuttled about here and there, crooning under their breath.

Lila and I had pushed ourselves onto the curve where a thick branch met the trunk of a tree, and the heavy fronds were covering us well. My black fur kept me hidden, and I was curled around Lila to help her blue scales not catch any errant light. More than that, we were small enough to be ignored.

A sudden soft cry of pain cut through the stillness of the night and my ears perked up. The rabisu below us froze and I got a good look at the ugly mug. They were all the same as far as I could see. Pale skin, open hole of a mouth with only fangs at the top that hung in a dual pair of perfect curves.

That open mouth stayed open as it scented the air. The slits for nostrils about the gaping hole were flared, though that didn't seem to mean much in terms of how big they actually were.

I looked at Lila. *You hear that?* I mouthed.

She nodded. But there was no additional cry.

The rabisu settled into his jerking movements again, working the area below us, flushing out some smaller prey which it didn't so much as take a swipe at. Though a bird flew in front of it and its face snaked out and bit the bird in half.

There wasn't even a moment for the bird to screech. Alive one second, dead the next, brightly plumed feathers floating around the two halves of its body. A flurry of movement and there were suddenly more rabisu there, digging at the bird's carcass, pulling the bits and pieces from it, cracking bones, spitting out feathers.

Lila grimaced and shook her head. *Nasty,* she mouthed.

I nodded and would have given her another quote to guess when that soft cry came again. The five rabisu below us turned as a unit and shot off down the long valley. A child's cry—I was sure of it. I unwound myself from Lila and shot forward along the branches, leaping from tree to tree.

Below us the rabisu took no note of my movements. I turned on the speed, using my claws to propel me forward faster to get ahead of the rabisu.

What had Jasten said? He had a family, children and wife killed. But what if one had been taken? What if he'd been looking for that last hope of a child still alive?

My heart clenched at the thought of a little one lost in the forest, looking for her father.

Terrified of the creatures hunting her.

"Sweet goddess, let us get there first," I whispered to myself as I leapt between trees.

Another cry, this one to the left.

"Lila, stay high!" I said as I spun and shot down the tree trunk I was on, hit the ground, and kept running. I wasn't worried about Lila. She'd keep safe above and give me any direction I needed.

Across the jungle floor I ran, the sounds of pattering feet somewhere behind me, stopping and starting in their weird jilting movements.

I kept my nose high, scenting the air, breathing it in as I frantically searched for the child. A whiff of shifter tickled my nose and I shot forward. She smelled a little like her father, and as I ran the scent grew stronger.

"Twenty feet behind!" Lila called out and a rabisu let out a shrieking cry.

Lila snarled, there was the sound of branches breaking, and then, "I'm okay. Get the kid."

I ducked under a low hanging bush and on the other side was a natural wall of the valley, made from a long-ago river cutting through and making this valley, leaving a place for the jungle to spring up. The wall rose high above our heads, straight up and here and there were openings that small animals no doubt used for cover. Three rabisu dug at the dirt wall, and the small crevice there that was about four feet high and only twelve inches wide.

Within that space a pair of shimmering blue eyes stared out at me from her hiding spot that was being chipped away with those incredibly long fingers of the monsters who would eat her given the chance. The dirt flew as they dug away, opening the crevice wider with each pass. The kid pressed backward, another cry slipping from her lips. She was running out of room, though, by the looks of it.

And there was no way to get her out of there without going through the rabisu.

There was no choice but to shift and fight them.

I took a breath and made the step between four legs to two, pulling the curved blade from my back.

*Kill them! Kill them!*

The song of the blade echoed through me as I swept the weapon forward, cutting down the first rabisu with an ease that lulled me.

I stepped to the left, took the second head, and the third rabisu turned and locked eyes with me. Stupid. I was being stupid, and I should have known it would not be so simple.

The image of monstrosity faded and Maks stood in front of me, smiling. "What are you doing?"

I blinked, my mind empty of what I was doing there. "Maks?"

He smiled and stepped closer, his hands reaching for me. "Of course."

*Treacherous lying filth. Kill him!*

The blade sung through me, the whispers demanding, pushing me . . . I lifted my blade. And he held up his hands. "Don't come any closer."

But his hands were hands I knew, hands I loved as they slid over my wrists and pulled me into his arms.

Someone was screeching and then Lila was on his shoulder, clawing his face. No, not Maks's face.

A rabisu.

I jerked backward, falling onto my ass, dragging the rabisu down with me. We rolled across the jungle floor, my arms tangled with the creature's unnaturally long limbs. The blade screamed in my head, just a long high-pitched wail of battle lust that I did not deny.

Twisting my wrist, I managed to get the blade between us, and up through the rabisu's heart. It jerked once as I stepped back from its now loose arms and swept the blade across its neck, taking the head.

A chirping in the jungle that was no bird had me running forward in a heartbeat. "Kid, we gotta go."

I reached into the crevice to grab the girl, and the little shifter bit my hand with a snarl. Of course, if I saw Maks, who might she have seen with the rabisu? Her father? Her mother?

I lay on my belly and wriggled into the crevice as far as I could, finding an ankle. "Sorry, kid. You'll thank me later."

I grabbed her around the ankle and yanked her onto her butt. She screamed, which only made me cringe as I dragged her out kicking and spitting, her eyes wild with fear. I scooped her into my arms, turned and shifted into my jungle cat form.

She quieted immediately and climbed onto my back as if she'd ridden a large cat a hundred times. Which she might have with her father. "Hang on." I leapt out of the small clearing as other rabisu slipped into it.

I wasn't fast enough, they saw us.

"Lila!"

"Go, go!" she yelled.

Yeah, easy enough. I raced through the jungle, my big cat form serving me well as I put distance between us and the rabisu. The problem was we needed a place to hide not only us but now a small child.

The chirping in the forest grew and the child on my back whimpered. "They know we're here."

"Hang tight," I grunted as I headed for a large

tree, vine-covered and ancient with the years it had seen, if the girth was any measure. I leapt straight up the trunk, pulling us up as quickly as I could. The little girl circled my middle with her legs and my neck with her arms. Her hold was something else as I struggled to breathe through her grip. Past the first three branches, I put as much leaves and vegetation between us and the ground as I could before I paused for breath.

Once we were thirty feet above the ground, I stopped and settled on a thick branch that would easily hold us both. The kid slid off the side of my back. I shifted to two legs and she cringed from me. I held up my hands and spoke in barely a whisper. "Quiet. I am not one of them. I won't touch you."

Still she cringed against the tree trunk. Fine by me, as long as there was no more screaming. A scuttling below us turned my attention downward.

Shapes circled the tree, and a rabisu could be seen about ten feet up the trunk.

"Fuck it all," I muttered.

Lila swept up to us. "They are surrounding the tree. What do you want to do?"

I looked to the small child. She couldn't have been more than five or six years old. Her black hair was in tangles around her head, and her eyes, so like her father's, glimmered with tears. "Can you shift?"

She stared hard at me. "Yes."

I drew a breath and pushed some of the alpha strength inherent in me into my command. "Shift."

She blinked, shook her head once, as if she would fight my words even as she felt the alpha power hit her. But it took only another moment and she shifted into a tiny jungle cat cub. "Lila. Take her north. If you have to, fly all the way to the end of the jungle and wait for me there."

Lila looked at me. "You can't fight them all, Zam."

A series of chirps fluttered around us. I shook my head and tucked my sword away. "I'm not. But I'm going to run, and I don't think she can keep up."

Lila flew to me and hugged me hard around the neck. "Be safe, sister of my heart."

I hugged her back. "Go."

She hopped over to the cub who cringed a little. "Hey, this will be fun. I'm going to hold you around the middle, and we're going to fly to the other side of this jungle."

The cub looked at her and she curled into Lila, for whatever reason, trusting the little dragon.

Lila scooped the cub up and flew upward, above the treetops. I watched them a moment until the chirping intensified. I was still going to kill a few of the little shits. I'd have to in order to get by them to the ground.

Only problem? A chirp to my left spun me as the rabisu launched at me from the tree next door.

It caught me around the waist, teeth aimed for my neck as we fell from the trees.

This was going to leave a bruise.

## 14

Chirping filled the jungle air as the rabisu and I fell through the tree, the branches getting in our way and bouncing us off to the side. Its fangs slid closer to me and it was all I could do to keep my one fist jammed up in its neck, holding its head back.

As we fell, I jerked us to one side and put the rabisu below me.

A split second later, we hit the soft vegetation littering the ground. Okay, maybe soft wasn't the right word. We came to a sudden stop and my body slammed into the rabisu's. Its teeth still snapped at me though its arms were limp. I rolled off it as the chirping picked up again, closing in on us. I forced my body to shift into my house cat form and scuttled away.

Chirping right in front of me and I slowly lowered myself to the ground, flat to my belly. The rabisu swept its head this way and that. Scenting the air. It paused right next to me, slitted nostrils flaring wide.

Fuck.

I gritted my teeth and bolted forward, racing away as the chirps went into a series of calls that echoed through the trees. Roosting birds shot into the night air, silent but for the pulse of their wings. A single moment of insight told me that the birds here had learned not to chirp. Learned not to make a sound.

Which meant every bird sound was a rabisu.

A volley of cries went up all around me.

So much for them not chasing down small prey. Then again, I'd stolen food from them and killed a few of their own. Who knew what kind of mind they had to understand that cost they bore because of me?

I sure as hell wasn't going to stop to ask.

Racing along the jungle floor, I dodged several sets of hands before the chirping eased. I didn't know how long the jungle stretch was, but it was long enough that I knew I wouldn't be able to cover it in one night as a house cat.

As a jungle cat, though, that was a different game altogether.

Keeping my speed up, I shifted from one cat to another as I ran. My strides lengthened and I more than doubled my speed as I used the simple pathways of the jungle. I found myself edging closer to the eastern dirt, sand, and rock wall of the valley as I ran. The sand sprinkled off like a spurt of fairy dust as my hip bumped it here and there. I hoped it wouldn't give them another way to track me.

At least that would keep my right flank protected. I didn't like how silently those rabisu fuckers moved when they wanted to, and I wouldn't put it past them to set up some sort of trap ahead of me.

An hour ticked by while the chirping behind me and to the left didn't slow, and it was a damn good thing I was in fighting shape. Even so, my lungs and muscles wouldn't hold up forever.

Either I was going to the end of this jungle, or I was going to need to find a place to hole up for a few hours.

The only problem I could see with that was that the rabisu had my scent and they were not giving up.

Not by a long shot.

Another hour, and I was slowing significantly and also beginning to think that maybe the jungle wasn't going to end. Maybe it just went on forever and ever. Maybe it was like Mamitu's castle that wouldn't allow me to leave until the rabisu gave me permission.

A chirp right behind me snapped me out of my thoughts and scooted me forward as the feeling of long spindly fingers sliding over my tail gave me a momentary burst of speed.

That was bad enough, but then came the line of rabisu in front of me, lined up like a game of Red Rover gone terribly wrong.

I didn't slow; maybe they thought I would.

I shifted mid-stride to two legs and reached for the weapon on my back. The blade came free with a sharp tang of metal on metal, clearing its scabbard with a ringing that cut through all the freaking chirping.

I put my back to the eastern wall of the valley, unable to continue north, and the rabisu came to me, crooning. Their faces turning into Maks. Turning into Ford and my brother, into Kiara and even Flora. Begging me not to hurt them. To let them hold me.

I let my eyes drift, peeking out through my lashes. That helped a little, and I gripped the sword handle harder.

*Now they will die.*

"Yes," I answered the sword and took my first swing. The heads of the rabisu fell one by one, their fingers reaching me, a set of teeth setting into my shoulder before I could kill that one. They fell, and I fought with everything I had.

More came.

Like a kicked nest of ants, they kept on coming and their songs intensified until all I saw was Maks.

Maks reaching for me. Begging me not to hurt him. Telling me he loved me.

And I cut him down.

I took his head.

I sliced through his belly.

I lopped off his arms and legs.

I knew it was not really him. I knew this was the song of the rabisu I had been warned about.

It didn't matter that I knew it was false. I saw his blue eyes lose the light in them time and again as I killed him. Them.

The ground soaked with blood at my feet until the dirt turned to mud.

I worked my way along the eastern wall, pushing forward even while I slaughtered them. I cut him down.

His head rolled from his shoulders so many times, my arms were numb from the blows reverberating through my bones. Teeth slid across my left arm as I blocked one version of Maks while I gutted another.

Tears streamed down my face, at first full of sorrow and then nothing but anger.

"I'll kill you all!" I screamed as I slashed at a rabisu who suddenly backed up, the image of Maks fading and the pale skin, white eyes and slitted nose all back in place.

The other rabisu stared and I stared back. What had stopped them? Surely, it wasn't the death I was inflicting.

Warmth on my head and neck made me want to look upward, but I didn't dare look away from them. I lifted my sword and the first rays of the sun reflected off the blade. The rabisu screeched and fled. I slumped where I was, breathing hard, my knees in the bloody mud.

I didn't close my eyes, but at the same time all I could see was Maks dying.

Goddess of the desert, what if Maks had tried to follow me, what if he'd been amongst them and I'd cut him down? My stomach lurched. I knew it wasn't true. They would have attacked him, and maybe killed him if he'd so much as set foot in the jungle.

Shaking hard, my muscles trembling, I stood once more and let the sun warm me.

There was a chirp here and there, but they faded as I listened for more.

I took a step out of the patch of sunlight and

then another and another until I was in a slow jog, still staying with my right flank against the eastern wall of the valley.

Another two hours slid by and finally the far north end of the jungle appeared, sunlight flooding everything. I stumbled out of the green undergrowth and was immediately assaulted by a flurry of blue scales as Lila slammed into my chest.

"Damn it, I thought I was going to have to go in after you!" She clutched at me a moment and then backed up. "Come on, we have to go. We need distance between us and this place before nightfall."

I bobbed my head but was struggling to breathe. "Bitten," I whispered and Lila squeaked as I fell forward, dropping to my hands and knees, barely catching myself from falling on my face. "Need to shift." I wasn't sure that a shift would heal the bite, but it would heal the wounds, and at the very least, Lila could pack me.

Stepping through the doorway in my mind that took me from two legs to four left me groaning and then whimpering as I breathed through the fire and pain. I could tell right away the bite hadn't healed properly, the venom still flowing sluggishly through my veins.

A small set of hands scooped me up and

clutched me hard to a shoulder far too little to be given any burden. "I'll carry her."

I blinked a few times as the girl hurried along. I bounced with each of her steps which left my stomach rolling but I wasn't going to complain. Much as it was a little humiliating to be packed along by a small child, in that moment, I wasn't going to tell her to put me down.

All three of us needed each other to get through this.

"Here, this will work," Lila said and I blinked my eyes open, not remembering when they'd closed. "Reyhan, put her down here."

The little girl—Reyhan—put me down gently. "The bites are bad. They killed my mother."

I forced one more shift to happen, rolled and puked up a little fluid. The nausea of the venom, the fatigue from fighting off the poison of the pillars, and multiple shifts close together was just too much.

"What have you got in your bag?" Lila dug at the leather bag on my hip.

"Nothing," I whispered.

I could only think one thing. Mamitu was wrong. I wasn't going to survive this.

Hands jerked at my bag and dumped out the contents. Reyhan bent over the items. "Here, my mother said this helps." She held up a package of herbs. "It needs to be a paste with water or wine to work."

The sound of Lila's wings, the snapping of twigs, the little girl singing softly to me. A lullaby, she sung a lullaby my own mother had sung to me. Her small hands patted my arm. "Lila is back."

There was a splash of water, then the feeling of a paste being pressed into the bite wounds that still bled, that still ached. My body jerked and danced as the thick green paste heavy with the scent of sage worked its magic on me and the sweet-smelling smoke filled my nose and eyes. Smoke . . . there shouldn't have been smoke. Should there?

I blinked and blinked through heavy lids at the fog—fog, not smoke—around us. This was not the dreamscape.

I was dying.

## 15

---

MAKS

The next morning, Maks rose early, and he and Batman were off and running before the sky lit up and the sun started its morning trek. And it was only luck that he turned his head to look to the north and saw the oncoming gray horse he knew all too well heading their way.

"She came to her senses," he said as he turned Batman north to intersect her. His heart lightened considerably as he galloped toward his mate.

He might want to strangle her, but in truth, he understood why she left. Which begged the question what had turned her around? Or had she found the Vessel of Vahab that quickly? Hope soared that the possibility was there. Maybe Zam was on her way back to Mamitu. She was good at finding things and had years of experience, as he'd pointed out.

Balder saw them coming and let out a neigh, and his rider . . . his rider fought him. Balder was having none of it, bucked once and threw Zam off. Maks squinted. "That's not Zam."

He leaned into Batman's neck and the horse threw himself into his strides, giving everything to get to his friend who still had one rein held by a now-irate man.

"Let him go!" Maks snarled as they slid to a stop. He was off Batman and circling Balder before they were even truly at a standstill. Pulling his weapon free, he tipped the blade at the dark-skinned man.

The man held up his hands. "Peace, I have no quarrel with you."

"You have my mate's horse, so unless your next words are—"

"Zam gave me the horse to ride back to Mamitu's," the man said. "The jungle is full of rabisu and they hunt anything larger than a bounding rabbit." He slumped a little where he stood. "She saved me."

Maks stared hard at the man in front of him. "You have a name?"

"Jasten Wilson. And you?"

"Maks."

Jasten held out his hand, palm up, and Maks took the proffered sign of peace. Particularly because Balder hadn't really been fighting his current rider. He also took note that Jasten had the same last name as Zamira and her brother. Interesting, but not really the point at that moment.

Maks looked to the north. "She went that way. Not east then."

"Through the jungle. If she's lucky." Jasten winced. "Sorry. I barely made it out alive, and I was there . . . I was searching for my family. What was left of them." His face tightened and there was a moment where his eyes glittered with tears, and he didn't have to say what they both knew. Jasten hadn't been able to save his family.

"I'm sorry for your loss," Maks said. The man in front of him knew more about this land than he did. "Is there any way around the jungle? Something faster that she might not have thought to ask about." Zam was kind of a point and shoot girl. She might have seen the jungle and locked on it.

Jasten looked hard at him. "Through the mines. They are as dangerous as the jungle, just in a different way. Dark, lots of pitfalls, and full of even more rabisu since it's their breeding grounds.

It wouldn't work for the horses. You think to catch her?"

"She'll make it through the jungle," Maks said, his eyes sliding to the north again. "But if I'm to catch her, I need to get ahead of her."

Jasten stared hard at him. "I'll go with you. I owe her my life. Perhaps she'll forgive me that debt if I keep you alive."

Maks knew that wasn't the real reason. The man in front of him had lost everything and had no worry that death might take him. He'd known men like Jasten, good men. Men who'd given up hope of ever living life to an old age. Men who sought battles like other men sought a whore.

"Then we ride to the mines," Maks said. He mounted and Jasten climbed aboard Balder, who stood patiently. Balder gave a snort and shook his head.

"You wouldn't go after her?" Maks said, his words sharp.

Balder jerked the reins out of Jasten's hands and stood facing the south. Maks twisted around and looked to the south. "What?"

Another toss of his head and a stomp of one foot, then Balder started to walk to the south.

Maks shook his head. "No, we're going after her."

Except that Batman turned and followed his

friend. Maks tried pulling the reins the other direction, tried to get his horse to listen, to no avail.

Jasten twisted around and looked at him. "We could walk."

Maks sighed and stared to the north as Batman took him south, following Balder. Damn unicorn. A part of his heart crumbled, all that hope that had built up gone on a puff of wind. Balder knew things Maks couldn't, and he trusted the equine on this. If Balder had left her behind willingly, then there was a reason.

"We'll go south. What is in that direction?"

Jasten shrugged and the horses picked up a steady trot, happy to be back together. "A whole lot of poor people and the ocean."

That caught Maks off guard. Not the ocean part, but the people part. "How many people is a lot?"

Jasten thought for a minute. "Millions."

Maks's jaw dropped. In his whole life, the most people he'd ever seen in one place was a few hundred. Not even a thousand. The desert he grew up in was sparse, harsh, ruled by Jinn and shifters where fights and battles to the death were just a part of life.

Millions of people, though, all living their lives . . . "Are they slaves?"

"Some, for sure. Most just scrape by, selling

wares and goods where they can, dying when they can't." Jasten frowned at Maks. "Why?"

Maks took one last look over his shoulder to the north, to where he could almost feel Zam on a journey he couldn't take with her. He thought about what she would do next, going through the lands of the next challenge. Then on to Asag. "If you were to ride as the crow flies from Mamitu's castle to the center of Asag's domain, how long would it take?"

"What are you thinking?"

Maks shook his head. "How long?"

"On a regular horse? I'd say a month."

A month, plus delays. "And to get to where these millions of people are?"

Jasten tapped his chin. "Couple of weeks maybe."

Maks's thoughts were propelling forward. "Do you have a map of Asag's domains? Or can you draw one?"

They pulled up short and Maks jumped off, followed by his new companion. Jasten crouched by the horses' hooves and sketched out a rough map. "We're here, the mountains are to the east, then through the forested lands of Pazuzu, then on to the fortress of Asag. To the far south is the ocean."

"Any rivers that feed into Asag's territory, and

are they used for trade?"

Jasten drew a quick line between the ocean and the center of Asag's territory. "The river of Naman. It is broad and while it flows with a few of the nastier beasties out there, it does carry a steady amount of trade into the beast's territory. Mostly food, cloth, some animals."

Maks tapped his finger on the river. "That is my way in. I will gain passage up the river, and I will wait for her there, at the center of the territory."

He wondered if he'd be stopped somewhere along the way. Then again, he wasn't trying to get to Asag.

He was trying to get to Zam. In that second, he saw the deviousness of the spell that the Beast from the East had placed on the land. If you wanted to get to him, to kill him, or take something that was his—like the hatchlings—there was no way in. If you wanted to visit your grandmother or sell some of your wares . . . that was acceptable. The spell would discern your intent and act accordingly. That was Maks's best guess.

Tricky, tricky demon.

Jasten stared at him, golden eyes flashing. "You don't know that she'll make it that far."

Maks snorted. "If we don't hurry, she'll beat me there. She is the granddaughter of the Emperor, a child of the desert and born to face strife and overcome it. I have more faith in her than I have in any soul this world has shown me."

He hadn't meant to say all that, but Jasten slowly nodded. "In the short time I knew her, I could see how you would believe that. She is . . . different, isn't she?"

Maks smiled and stood. "She is everything I never knew I would follow with everything I am. She showed me what it is to be a true alpha, to be a leader, to hold to bonds of family chosen and not born into. She will change this world."

Jasten rubbed his arms and was quiet a moment. He stood and leapt up in a single bound onto Balder's back. "Then we'd better get you on a ship. Goddess only knows what this woman of yours would do if you showed up late to her party."

Maks laughed. "She'd have drunk all the țuică and started without us." He followed, hopping up onto Batman's back and urging the horse into a gallop, feeling the need to move.

He had to get to Zam, and the only way to be at her side when the time came was to beat her there. Maks kept his mind clear of any intent. Thoughts of other things, of promises to keep and things to do could happen after he was settled and waiting for Zam.

One thing at a time, and until then, he would

pray to the gods of the desert and storm that she made it there in one piece.

The only problem was there was a storm that answered his prayers, just not in the way he'd have thought. In a way that changed everything in a split second.

The fog surrounding me was some sort of limbo, I was sure. I was not quite dead from the rabisu bite, not quite back with the living with the paste that Lila and Reyhan had put on my wounds.

I stood and did a slow circle, looking for an indication of where I was, or if there was a way back to being . . . alive?

"Hello?" I called out into the fog and the world seemed to split down the middle, right between my feet. To the left of me was darkness, utter and complete, a night so inky black that even my eyes would not see through it. It bled into the gray fog that surrounded me and a thin strip that ran north and south of me. That fog blended to the right of me into a brightness that was beyond sunlight and fire. A pure light that I'd only seen in electrical storms with the power of lightning behind the illumination. I shaded my eyes.

A figure approached from the brilliance and a laugh on my left turned my head.

A figure approached from the darkness.

They stopped about ten feet from me on either side. The figure on the right stood tall, straight, and her hair was braided to one side. Her clothing was a simply cut dress, clean, brilliantly silver.

The figure on my left was . . . he stood half hunched over, his body twisted yet still muscular. Eyes of night stared out at me from under a mop of hair. His skin was dark red, reminding me of Mamitu's dress.

"This is the one?" he growled.

"Yes," the woman said, her voice gentle and kind.

"She's rather scrawny."

"Should the bite take her, the creature she'd become would be a horror beyond anything we've ever seen."

He tried to take a step closer but couldn't seem to get past the fog. "She's dying. We'd better hurry it up then."

"Yes. But we have the power to send her back." Her voice wrapped around me and I sunk to my knees as surely as if she'd bashed them with a bat.

"You're sure?" he grumbled. "Seems a waste when she'll likely just die again. But you're right, the monster she'd be with rabisu blood pounding in her would be a shit show. We've enough of those right now without adding another."

And then his voice wrapped around me and I was tossed back into my body, Lila thumping on my chest with her entire weight, jumping up and down and using her wings to propel her. I coughed and managed to push her off as I rolled to the side.

Little hands pressed a cup to my lips. "Drink the water with the herbs in it. My mama said always to drink this if you got bit by a rabisu."

I gulped down the water, parched from the run, the venom, from everything in the last twenty-four hours. The taste of mint and sage lingered on my tongue, a hint of something else that washed away some of the fatigue and the headache I only noticed as it left me. All of that was what I focused on because the conversation between the light and the dark was too much for me in that moment.

"Thank you, Reyhan," I whispered.

She smiled shyly and sat beside me, tucking her long dark brown hair behind her ears. "Are you better now?"

I blinked up at her, then looked to Lila as she hurried back to me. I pushed to where I could sit up and rest my back against the wall of . . . a cave? And the light was fading. Again.

"Yes, I'm better. How long was I . . ." I wanted to say gone, but that wasn't right. Almost dead was closer to the truth. "Out for?"

"Most of the day, and then you stopped breathing," Lila said, crawling into my lap and placing her front feet on my chest so she could stare into my eyes. "Your eyes are no longer dilated, that's good."

I nodded and drank down the dregs of the cup of water. "Check the wounds, please."

Lila scooted around and checked out the backs of my arms. "They are clear, no red lines and the flesh is almost healed. Like it happened weeks ago." She bobbed around to the front of me. "Those herbs are amazing."

I didn't want to say anything in front of the little girl. I managed to pull my cloak off and laid it on the ground. "Here, Reyhan, you keep it warm for me. I'll see if I can get us food."

Lila followed me out of the narrow cave, and I motioned for her to stay quiet. "You stick close to the girl. We need something for a door."

Lila stared up at me. "You sure you're feeling okay? That was a ridiculously fast turnaround. Even for you."

I nodded. "I'll explain later after the girl is

asleep. Right now, we need a barrier. You can't tell a rabisu to fuck off, if you aren't even in a proper house."

Because that was what Mamitu had said. Don't invite them in. I didn't think she meant only your body. But your home.

We were at the mouth of the valley, high above an open plain. Not of desert, but of grass and rolling hills. Far below me a herd of horses grazed, a blend of colors that were nothing short of breathtaking, from the palest of creams, to the brightest coppers, gold, black, and even a few with spotted patterns. "Balder, you'd love this," I whispered.

For just a moment, I turned and looked to the south as if I could feel him there. Maybe I could. It wouldn't surprise me.

Maybe we could come back here after this was all done.

I smiled to myself and the image of the woman in white and the monster in dark red skin wiped that smile right off my face. I turned away from the view and scrounged until the light was fading.

There was nothing to use for a door. Fear made my heart trip. I strode back to the cave, the stone walls of it thicker than the one that Reyhan had found herself in on her own, hiding from the rabisu.

I looked at her sleeping soundly on my cloak.

The only thing that could even pretend to be a door. I pulled my bedroll out and spread it on the hard ground, then carefully transferred the sleeping kid. I picked up my cloak and held it up. "This is all we got, Lila. This is our home, and this cloak is the door."

"Works in the desert," she pointed out as she flew up, snagging the edge of it and helping me stuff it into the top portion of the cave opening. I pinned down the bottom of it with rocks, holding it in place.

"You think it will be enough?" Lila asked quietly.

"No idea," I said and slumped to the ground. The bag that Mamitu gave me bumped on my hip and I opened it. Hunks of soft wax were wrapped in cloth with a note pinned to it.

"For your ears, to stem the spell of the rabisu," I read out loud.

I rolled the wax out, took a portion and put it in each of my ears, then did the same for Lila and even the sleeping Reyhan. "This would have been handy earlier."

Lila curled up next to the sleeping child, yawned and ducked her head down. I leaned against the side wall of the cave and stared at the lightly fluttering cloak that was pretending to be a door. Cloth was going to hold back the rabisu?

I did not have much faith in it, despite my words to Lila and the girl. Let them sleep a little while, rest, while they believed they were safe. My throat tightened.

Maks was out there, maybe following us through the jungle. I was no fool to believe that he wouldn't at some point try to get to us.

A tremor rippled through my jaw as I held back tears. Blame it on the fatigue, blame it on the near-death experience, but my emotions ran hot under my skin and my eyes leaked as a result.

I turned my head, trying to hear something outside of the beat of my own heart and the loudness of my breath inside my head.

But the wax blocked off everything from one of my most acute senses and one I relied on to stay safe. From the breathing of the two sleeping ones, to the rustle of the cloth I knew was there, to even the wind through the trees outside. I felt naked, exposed, without hearing what was coming for us.

I could always put the wax back in.

With a grimace, I pulled the thick stuff from my ears, and the sounds about us rushed through me.

The flap of the cloak, the whisper of little animals going about their nightly routines, Lila mumbling in her sleep for another sip of țuică. That last one made me smile and I turned my head to look at her curled in the crook of the child's arms.

The sound of long fingers sliding against the cloak behind me stilled my movements and my breath. A soft chirp of the rabisu sounding us out. Lila and Reyhan were silent, safe in their dreaming.

I turned my head to see the shadow of a much larger body, thicker, heavier than the other rabisu. My heart picked up speed, dancing in my chest, as if by sheer force of that drum, it could make me run from this thing outside the cave.

"I hear your breathing change in there, shifter. I smell your fear. Why don't you come out and speak with me, or better yet, let me in?" The serenading words called to me, but not because I wanted to let the fucker in.

No, that curiosity was a part of me wanting to see this new rabisu despite the fear. This was not the mindless mob of ants that had come for us, trying to overwhelm us with numbers. This was something different. Something far more dangerous.

"You have a name?" I made myself move closer to the cloak. I lifted a hand and placed it on the handle of the sword strapped to my back, palm slick with nervous sweat I could not stop from dripping down my arms.

*Death . . . that one is death. Kill him.*

Much as I agreed with the whispers of the weapon, I ignored her pleading. I would not be so much as moving an inch of the cloak disguised as a door. I would hold this place till morning if it killed me.

Strike that, not a great phrase to use right then.

The rabisu slid its fingers across the cloak again, not tearing it, but testing the hold of the material. "You may call me . . . Steve."

I blinked a few times, not sure I heard him right. "I'm sorry, did you say STEVE?"

"That is a strong name, a name that—"

My laughter cut him off. I took my hand from the blade handle and bent at the waist as I roared with it, unable to contain the ridiculousness of this monstrous rabisu claiming the name of my ex-husband, the biggest douche and dumbest shifter of them all. Yeah, so my choice in men in the past had been poor. But it saved me from the fear that had been eating me up from the inside.

Steve. The idiot would call himself Steve.

It took me a moment to gather myself. "You could not have chosen a worse name from my history, but the Steve of my past is dead, killed not once, but twice, and only after he fell headfirst into a pile of shit. So perhaps your choice of names is fitting. If you want to follow his lead."

The rabisu crouched close to the cloak. "Your scent has changed. You do not fear me. Why is that?"

I glanced at Lila and Reyhan, still asleep through my belly laughter. That was good. I found myself drawing closer to the cloak, to that space where nothing but the light material separated us. "I would ask you the same question. Why do you not fear me?"

The creature snorted. "I am king here. I fear nothing."

"The sun. I'm betting you fear the sun like all of your little friends," I said.

"They are my children, and you've been slaughtering them," he growled and let out a series of chirps. Somewhere in the distance he was answered, a hundred times over until the sound swelled like the rising of a storm.

I gritted my teeth, fear finding me once again. Night had barely fallen. We had at least ten hours of darkness, and I was no fool as to think I could hold the narrow doorway that long should they rush us.

I had to buy time, and that meant engaging with this . . . Steve.

"Your children attacked me, *Steve*." I adjusted my crouch so I was ready to move if he came through the doorway. "And they were attacking a defenseless child."

Steve let out a series of chirps that sounded almost like a purr. "That child is far from defenseless. Her death would be better with us than with the one who would take her for his bride."

Bile rose in my throat. "What did you say?"

"You do not know?" Steve's chuckle was dark. "I find myself wanting to speak with you. The first to look past their fear in so long that I could have a conversation. Years have passed since such a time."

"You mean your children don't speak with you?" I paused. "Shitty father, huh?"

A snort came from the other side of the cloth. "They are my spawn, and they have no will but my own, you stupid chit. They have no consciousness."

I let myself sit, easing the muscles in my legs. "Ah, so you really don't give a shit that I killed them then."

There was silence from the rabisu. "They are mine to do with as I would."

"Tell me about the one that would take the girl," I said.

"If I tell you, will you come out to see me?" the rabisu whispered. "Make me a promise that I could see the face of the one who is engaging my mind."

I twisted my face. "I will lift the cloth near to the morning light if you talk with me until then."

Perhaps it was a terrible idea. It might very well have been. But how many more nights did we have going through the territory of these creatures? What if I could gain us another day just by talking, not fighting?

I would take that chance to save my body from another battle and rest a little.

"All right, Steve. Let's talk."

## 17

S itting in the cave with a cloak pretending to be a door, I didn't know what to expect from "story time" with a parasitic rabisu named Steve. But let's just say I didn't hold out hope for anything intellectual.

I was wrong.

I was so wrong.

"You want to know about the power of the child you hide from us? Why we took her? Why we would kill her?" Steve breathed the words through the cloth, his fingers touching the edges here and there. Testing.

"It's still our door, fucker. Stop playing with it," I snapped.

He chuckled. "Yes, yes, the simple act of belief. It is a power that too few understand."

I sat to the side of the doorway and I could just see the edges of his body. Like the shadows had shown me, there was not much similarity between him and the rabisu that had chased us through the jungle. His body seemed heavy with muscle, his fingers long but not wildly so. That was all I got in flashes as he paced the other side of the cloth. "Tell me of this world I do not understand. I am from the western desert and the eastern realm is unknown to us."

That seemed to give him pause. "You come from that which is forbidden? And you come here without knowing the dangers?"

"I come for a promise given, to find the hatchlings of the dragons, to free them to go to their mothers. And along the way, I stumbled onto the girl." I shrugged. Though he could not see my movement, I had a feeling his hearing was as good as mine. "I have a tendency to find the unwanted, the broken, the cast away."

He lowered himself to a crouch. "That one is not unwanted. But let me explain this world to you, and then to the girl."

His voice took on a tone that told me he had spun tales before. Melodic, hypnotizing, and more than a little easy on the ears. More than that, as he spoke, I saw the images come to life in front of my eyes like a moving story.

"When the walls first rose, when the Emperor was first cut off from the human world, madness reigned between the western and eastern walls. The western wall bordered forests and arctic cold. The eastern wall bordered a seething mass of humanity, much of which was trapped behind it before they realized what had happened.

"The Emperor . . . he was strong enough to hold the entire realm, but he wanted security. So, he found old texts, old runes, that told him how to raise an army of demons. He went into the depths of darkness to find them, to bring them to life in the flesh. They possessed his generals. Warped their minds, stealing what was left of their souls and ruling completely.

"He got more than he bargained for—not the army he wanted, but a rival that had no care for his life, nor for the lives of those he now rules. Asag was the first of the Gallu demons that Shax brought into the light. He claimed the eastern realm with an iron fist, destroying any who would defy him."

The images flashed in front of my mind, great battles, explosions of magic, creatures that were beyond my imagination as they slammed into one another. And the Jinn . . . they fought for the Emperor and even that was not enough. The rabisu fought for the demon, Asag. He sat astride a massive bird with wings of red . . . no, with wings that dripped blood from those he'd killed. He was taller than any man I knew, his body built muscle upon muscle. In the midst of the battle I watched, he turned his head and looked at me.

Blue eyes, eyes a color I'd seen once before, stared at me.

"Maks." I whispered his name and the scene shattered. I lifted my hands to shade my eyes from a scene that broke apart around me.

Steve tapped his nails against the ground, drawing my attention back to him.

"The battles raged for three years. Millions died. In the end, the Emperor struck a deal with Asag. That the western desert and the eastern desert would be forbidden from one another. There would be no history for either and they would remain separate for as long as time stood. As by your demeanor, I can only assume the Emperor kept his part of the bargain. He wiped the memories of his Jinn, and any who knew of this place."

"Let me guess, this Asag did not?" I drawled.

Steve snorted, a distinctly human moment I did not like. "Of course not, he's a demon. Those who deal with demons deserve to be fooled."

His words chilled me more than a little, because if I were to guess, I'd say he and his rabisu flock were demons of a different sort. "What happened next?"

"Asag used the Jinn he'd captured to create weapons for him. To trap those powers that he wanted to use for his own purposes."

"Like Mamitu," I said.

"Yes, the queen of fate and destiny is one such. The king of plagues is another. Both had stood with the Emperor against Asag, but in the last moment, claimed they were only undermining the Emperor's strength from behind enemy lines. It was, as the humans say, a 'Hail Mary' and Asag chose to spare them. If binding them to his fate for eternity could be called sparing them."

Again, another series of images rolled in front of my eyes. Mamitu and the man with the short dark beard that I knew was Pazuzu on their knees in front of the monstrously huge Asag. What looked like necklaces were laid over their heads. The amulet on each was the crescent moon on fire. They bowed their heads, and the necklaces slithered around their necks and sunk into their flesh.

Mamitu fell to the side, convulsing, and Pazuzu shook where he was, barely able to remain upright.

I blinked and stared at the cloth between me and the rabisu with the unfortunate choice of names. "So they are slaves to him."

"As am I," Steve said. "All who walk this land are the slaves of Asag. We do his will, and he sees through us that which we see."

"Why would you tell me this?"

He was quiet a moment. "I find you interesting. You do not fall to my voice as any other would. I am . . . curious about you. Mind you, you will still die before the night falls, so I feel no fear that my speaking to you will cause concern for me and mine."

I rolled my eyes. "So much bravado from one who cannot part a curtain."

His laughter surprised me. "So much mouth from one whose death is signed in the stars."

I closed my eyes a moment, thinking. "I have questions."

"Ask. We have hours together to get to know one another before you die," he said, as silky smooth as ever.

"Why did he steal the hatchlings?" I pushed the heel of my boot into the ground, digging a small trench. "What purpose could he have for the dragons? I mean, I'm assuming it wasn't the obvious wanting a cool dragon to ride through the skies to terrorize your people. The theft has been too systemic and too far-reaching for there to be anything so simple as that, at least in my mind."

Steve tapped his fingers against the curtain.

"You are correct. He took them for the power they bring. And for the fear of what could happen if he didn't."

I frowned. "I don't understand."

The rabisu stood and paced in front of the cloak/curtain/door. "He is a demon, and as such, there are many things tied to his life, rule, and potential death. Symbols and signs that predict he might fall obsesses him. One story he believes is how he will survive any who come for his life. It is why the girl child is in danger. He believes that the blood of the innocent wards off danger. He'd drain her blood and use it to bring another demon to his party."

"But why her? You seem to think it was a specific reason."

"Because she is a shifter's child, and a child of the desert through her bones. That is a power not found often now in the eastern world."

My frown did not ease and I fired another question off at him. "What kind of symbols does he look for?"

He was quiet a moment. "The whispers of a prophecy that he burns down at every chance, are barely even a whisper now, and only because I have been alive so long, do I know any of them. Now they are fragmented and partial at the best of times. A unicorn that is not. A dragon that cannot be seen. When the Vessel of Vahab is broken, the hatchlings shall bear an army to protect him. A rider that sings the song of Lilith. The last of the Emperor's line comes to pay their final respects to Asag. None of it fits. Together, they are but pieces of prophecy far too long gone to understand."

I swallowed hard, couldn't manage any spit and reached for my waterskin. Sweet baby goddess, was this why we needed to come here? Was there more at work than the dragon hatchlings? I took a heavy drag on the liquid, letting it ease down my all-too-tight throat. "And nothing more of that prophecy?"

"You . . . you understand it?" Steve twisted around, the cloak rippling with his movement. "Do you understand what it would take to stop him? I hear it in your voice that these words mean something to you."

"Why would you want him stopped?" I asked. "What matter would it be to you?"

He snorted. "You think this is how my people look? These monstrosities designed for fear and death? You think this is how I look? I am a monster created, but I came from something else. Something fairer, something that adored the sun and all its warmth and now I am consigned to darkness and death. If you know the name of the rider, or the last of the Emperor's line . . . tell me now. I will give you safe passage through this place to wherever it is you think to go. For a name."

This was one of those moments that perhaps I dared too much. Perhaps I should have thought more about what I would do or say before I did it. But my heart was pounding and the twist in my belly told me that I had to follow my instincts. I found my hand reaching up to touch the sword because it was the one part that didn't fit. Her voice whispered through me.

*Lilith.*

I closed my eyes. "Fuck me." Of course, it was the blade of some far flung prophecy. Damn it all to hell and back. Yet I wasn't truly surprised. There was always something pulling me forward, some injustice to make right and I knew why. Desert guardian, desert cursed. This was my life.

I pulled back from standing, a decision forming even as I spoke. "I will tell you what I know. The rider that carries Lilith," I reached up again without meaning to, as if called to her handle, and touched the sword handle on my back. She all but hummed under my fingers, a merry tune of death and destruction, "is in these lands."

A sigh escaped him. "Then we are close to freedom if he is on his way to Asag. You have my word that I will not harm you or those who travel with you for this news."

Silence, and I thought of Maks who would at some point track me. He wouldn't leave me to see this through on my own, no matter that I left him a note, no matter that his life would be in danger.

"There is another, a man who will be following me," I said. "He rides a black horse and has blue eyes—"

"The black rider comes too then." Sorrow leached into the rabisu's voice. "Then all shall yet come to pass."

My fingers itched. I wanted to see this creature's face, to see if the sorrow was put on or just an act to draw me out. I clamped my fingers together and sat on them. "What of the black rider?"

"Not that it matters to you, but the black rider will save Asag."

I shook my head. "No. He wouldn't do that. You have to believe me, he would not help a demon!"

"I cannot give him safety. If he passes through our way, I will destroy him."

## 18

I blew out a breath and pushed the curtain/cloak/door of our temporary cave abode aside and stepped into the darkness of night, and the goddess only knows how many fucking rabisu were waiting for me. Trusting the word of the head rabisu named Steve. Steve. Why was it always motherfucking Steve?

The rabisu tipped his head to the side. Like I'd already figured, he was muscular, tall, and moved with a lethality that made the mobs of smaller, slender rabisu look like children. Then again, he'd said as much. He had a normal nose and eyes, and his face was very human-looking despite the over-sized fangs hanging from his upper jaw.

"You trust me?"

"No," I said. "But I cannot allow you to kill him

if he comes through. He is my mate. I need you to see me to understand me." I looked him straight in the eye. "Let him pass. If it comes to a moment where he needs to die for the safety of the world," I pulled my blade clear of its sheath, "then I will be the one to do it."

Steve put his hands on his hips like a peeved father figure. "You would kill your own mate."

"It has come to that before," I said. "But if you do not agree to this, then you and I will fight right here, previous promises be damned."

His tongue snaked out to rub up and down the length of one fang. I grimaced. "That's creepy as fuck. Don't do that."

Steve's eyes widened and he laughed. "You think I don't know that? You think I don't know how creepy and nasty I am?"

"If you did, you wouldn't do that." I flicked the tip of my sword up so it pointed at his chest and his eyes drifted to the blade, widening farther.

"Where did you get that blade?"

Ah, shit. Of course, he'd recognize it. I couldn't put it away, and now I was all but outing myself as part of the prophecy he'd just told me. I didn't lower it, though.

His eyes swept over me and narrowed. "Who are you?"

"What does it matter now?" I flicked the sword

at him and the whisper of her voice called me to do more than test his flesh with the edge.

"You are the one."

"No. I'm not," I said. "I am here to save the hatchlings, that is all, nothing more."

Lila took that moment to poke her head out around the cloak edge. "Zam? Who are you talking too—ahhh!" She screeched and shot into the air so she was eye level with me.

I held a hand to her and pulled her to my shoulder while the rabisu stared hard at me. "You are the one. The last of the bloodline of the Emperor."

"How did he know that?" Lila whispered, and I grimaced while he grinned like a fool.

"He didn't," I said, feeling defeated that he knew. I didn't want to point out to him that I had a bunch of half-aunt witches who lived in a swamp. So the prophecy was off at best. "Lila, meet Steve."

She blinked a couple times, her long lashes dusting her cheeks. "Does he know that's a sucky name?"

He was still grinning, his fangs clearly visible. He bowed at the waist. "The rabisu will bother you no more. But to where do you ride? I can give advice on the safest direction."

Lila's claws dug into me. "I feel like I missed a

hell of a conversation. And it makes me nervous that he's being helpful."

"You have no idea," I said. "But let's start with this. We go to find the Vessel of Vahab in order to gain permission to cross the mountains into Pazuzu's lands, and from there into Asag's territory."

Steve paced in front of us, stroking his bare chin. "You will face one more monster, and then there is the issue of where the vessel is. The natural boundaries that stand between you and your prize are rather . . . difficult. Mountain wolves. The river of death, on and on."

"I know the where of it," I said. "So tell us about the monster."

The rabisu chirping faded as they all slid away except the one. He crouched and motioned for us to join him as if we were sitting around a fire. His eyes flicked over me and Lila multiple times. I wasn't sure if it was hunger or something else.

"The Nasnas. Its touch dissolves flesh like acid, and it lives in the river in which you will find the vessel waiting at the bottom. Reptilian creatures swim the river constantly searching for food, their bellies always empty, their mouths full of teeth."

He stood and looked to the east. "Though it might not feel it to you, the night has gone."

I shook my head. "This has barely been an hour, no more."

Steve bowed again at the waist. "No, the hours have passed, and you withstood my call that entire time. Well done, last of the Emperor's line. May you find your way to Asag and end his life."

He backed up, still in a perfect bow as the sun crept over the edge of the valley, bathing the world in light. And in a blink, he was gone, and Lila and I were alone.

She peppered me with questions as I stumbled back into the cave, answering her with all I'd just learned. Even with that distraction of giving her the information, I was shocked that the night had gone by, that even though I'd fought the pull of the rabisu, his voice had still hooked into me enough to fool me with the passage of time.

The girl sat up as we came in, stretched and blinked up at me. I reached over and pulled the wax from her ears. "Come. We need to hurry."

Time was slipping by. We ate a meager meal as we walked, and as the girl's legs began to falter, I scooped her onto my back. The valley below us was still full of horses, and a thought that maybe there would be traders here, and that we could take a horse to hurry our speed, flitted through me.

That was until we drew closer to the herd and

they lifted their heads from the lush grass of the plains.

Horns sparkled, catching the morning light. A whinny trumpeted from the lead stallion, his coat brilliantly white and shimmering as he barreled toward us.

I did the only thing I could.

I went to my knees and bowed my head, tucking the girl and Lila under my arms.

"Run!" Lila squirmed and I shook my head.

"No, trust me. Running will only set him off further."

She whimpered and I held myself still, folded over them both.

The thunder of hooves thrummed through my veins and I waited. Not because I couldn't have fought, but because . . . how, how could I ever look Balder in the eye again if I had slain, or even hurt, one of his kind? Assuming I survived, that is. Mamitu had said there were fewer than a dozen unicorns left, and I could see them now, mixed in with the horses here. I couldn't hurt one. And I had to trust that a unicorn would know we were no threat to them.

Dirt and grass spewed around us as the stallion slid to a stop, screamed his battle cry again and then slammed his front hooves into the ground in front of my face.

A muzzle grazed the back of my neck, hot breath fluttering my hair.

There was no voice from him. I held up a hand, palm up and my head still lowered as far as I could while hunching over the other two. "Hello."

He snorted and pressed his muzzle into my palm and licked it.

I lifted my head slowly and stared into the eyes of what could have been Balder's brother. Or maybe father.

His coat was solid white, not an ounce of dappling left in his hide, and his eyes were as dark as the color of my hair. "We seek passage." I lifted myself so he could see Reyhan and Lila tucked under me.

He lowered his head, horn flashing dangerously close to my eye, then lower to brush against Lila's back, then across the little girl's forehead. Never fully touching, just gazing them.

He stepped back and let out a low snort, and I breathed a sigh of relief. No words were given, he just turned his back on us and trotted away.

Good enough. I stood and Lila shot into the air. "I'll see what it looks like ahead."

I took Reyhan's hand and started walking as if we hadn't almost been skewered on the end of a horn.

"Would he have hurt us?" she asked, her eyes so round they seemed to fill her whole face.

"If we'd meant harm, yes," I said. "Animals are perceptive, and unicorns more than any other."

I hurried us along and she asked no more questions, her hand tight in my own. At some point, I needed to find a place for her, a place to be safe, but I didn't think that was going to happen. What place of safety could there be in this world where rabisu roamed and a demon ruled?

The long grass swished around us as we moved at a good clip. I kept my eyes on the goal, ever northward, not allowing myself to look too much at the unicorns. I wanted to stay, hell, I could have stood there for hours and just drunk them in with my eyes.

A few stood in our direct path and I bowed my head to them and went around them, not willing to disturb them.

From ahead of us, I watched as Lila suddenly turned and made a beeline back toward me. "Mountain wolves!" she screamed. "A pack of them!"

The unicorns bolted for the far end of the field. We'd never outrun the wolves on foot.

A young unicorn swept by us and I tossed Reyhan onto his back despite the widening of the young colt's eyes. "Hold tight!" I pointed a finger at the colt. "And do not buck her off!"

Everything was happening too fast. We needed to get to the river, which was on the other side of these plains.

I could pull my sword.

I could shift into my jungle cat form.

The cat might draw them more and that was enough for me. I ran toward the oncoming wolves, shifting mid-stride.

From two legs to four, I picked up speed, and caught my first glimpse of the wolves. There was nothing ordinary about them. They were massive, their size making me think of the white wolf.

And there were five of them.

I didn't have to yell at Lila to have my back or tell her to work with me.

I crouched in the long grass, flattening to my belly. The lead wolf raced toward me, and I held my ground.

"Wait," Lila called out, "wait." Her voice was all I listened for over the drums of my own heart.

"NOW!"

I leapt up with all I had and slammed into the oncoming wolf, rolling us through the air even as I ripped his throat out with my teeth. We hit the ground and I bounded to the left at the next wolf, sending him ass over teakettle, raking his body with my back feet, looking for that sweet spot of disembowelment. My left foot caught his soft underbelly and gouged out the flesh.

Teeth snapped onto my right shoulder and jerked me off the wolf, but he was already done, intestines flowing into the sweet grasses as he struggled to breathe.

Three wolves left.

All they saw was a large cat and encircled me, muzzles rippled up as they snapped and lunged at me, their jaws chattering. They were thin, ribs showing through their thick gray pelts, their teeth flashing as they snarled.

To come at a herd of unicorns was no small thing, and starvation had driven them to it.

I circled with them while I kept them at bay with swipes from my own claws.

They did not expect an attack from above.

Lila dropped onto the back of the one on my right and clamped on hard at the back of his neck where he couldn't reach her. Teeth and claws and a screeching so goddess-awful that my fur puffed up all over my body.

As a companion wolf lurched to help his friend, or maybe just eat the small dragon, I stepped toward him.

Shifting quickly back and forth between two and four legs was tiring, but I held it together. I shifted, grabbed the blade from my back, and brought it down on the skull of the wolf, splitting it in half.

That one went down, but my back was to the final wolf, and I knew it was the mistake that was going to cost me dearly. I managed to get my forearm up around the back of my neck as teeth clamped down. I was driven to the ground, face first in the dirt and he shook me like a limp rag.

Lila was screaming but the ground had my attention. The ground and the feel of hooves as they thundered closer. I closed my eyes, unable to do anything but pray that help was indeed coming. Seconds past, the teeth pressed in hard on my arm that was barely holding him at bay.

The wolf on top of me suddenly relaxed his hold on me, howled and snarled, the sound intense with its jaw wrapped around the back of my neck. A scream of pain from him, and then the body of the wolf slumped onto me, pinning me to the ground.

Lila's voice was there like the buzzing gnat she'd been called as a child, frantic and freaking the fuck out. I mumbled something but it was hard to speak with my face in the dirt. The body of the wolf was rolled off me and I went to my hands and knees, brushed off my face and then pushed to my feet.

Bite marks marred my arm, there were holes on the back of my neck, but none were deadly, and for once, it looked like there was no poison in them. Go me for being bit by something non-venomous. The bones were bruised, but nothing was broken either.

Reyhan bobbed along on the back of the filly I'd shoved her on. "Are you okay?" she asked.

I nodded. "I am. Come, we have to go." I motioned for her to get off and she did as I asked, sliding to the ground. A small part of me wished I could leave her with the herd, but they had no way to properly care for her. For the time being, she was still with us.

I looked up at the stallion in front of me. "Thanks. You saved my bacon."

He shook his head, mane flipping from side to side and an image flowed between us.

Of me riding him into battle. Of the bodies of monsters I couldn't identify under our feet. A banner in my one hand.

I swallowed hard. "You have a herd to care for. More wolves could come. Goddess only knows what else this place harbors. And there aren't many of you left."

He went to one knee and bowed his head to me. One more image, one that felt like a story from long before, hit my mind.

Of a colt that he'd bid farewell to, a colt that became my horse, and that I'd left behind to save him from the jungles of the rabisu.

"You . . . *are* his father," I whispered, daring to touch his neck. He shivered and then stood upright again. A quick bob of his head and a sharp whinny that brought the rest of the herd close.

A second younger stallion stepped up, his coat not unlike that of Balder's, dappled gray all over, and the same soft eyes. "A brother?"

The elder stallion touched the tip of his horn to his son's, and the herd wheeled away, leaving me there with a seriously unexpected mount.

I stared at him. "I'm riding into certain danger."

He bobbed his head, a move so like Balder, it tugged at my heart.

"We could all die," I pointed out.

Another bob.

"It looks like I'm going to face off with Asag at some point."

He reared up on his back legs and pawed at the sky, and then dropped once more to a single knee.

"Okay, long as we got that out of the way," I said and went to his side. His back was broader than Balder, and his muscling . . . heavier, thicker. I took a hold of his mane and pulled myself up. He waited and I held out a hand to Reyhan. She took hold of my fingers and I lifted her to sit in front of me.

The stallion stood and there was an electrical sensation that flowed over my seat and legs, locking us onto his back.

"That tickles," Reyhan whispered.

"Lila. You better get over here." I held my hand out and she shot to my wrist just as the stallion leapt forward with more power and speed than even Balder carried. I tucked Lila under my cloak and we raced across the plains toward the north and the dangers that waited.

"We need to walk today," Maks said. "Batman's knee is swollen."

Three days had passed as he and Jasten rode hard for the south. They went as fast as Batman could go, and even then, Maks knew they were pushing the older horse too hard.

On the morning of the fourth day, Batman was lame.

Maks smoothed a hand over the horse's swollen knee, an old injury that hadn't flared up in a long time. Not since . . . well, not since the hunt for Dragon's Ground. "Okay, old man. We'll give it a slow day."

Jasten fussed about with Balder's saddle, getting it just right. Maks had to give the man credit, he took good care of the horse that had been loaned to him. Balder nuzzled his rider all over, looking for oat balls no doubt.

"We are coming up to a small town. We could see about trading him?" Jasten offered.

Maks's jaw ticked. Not out of anger with Jasten, because the suggestion was one any normal person would make. The horse was lame, and they had a long way to ride yet.

"We'll see what there is in the market," Maks managed to say without spitting the words. He smoothed his hand over Batman's hide. He was far older than most horses, having survived because of the magic Balder had shared with his stablemate.

Leading along his four-legged friend, Maks started south once more, in part wanting to hurry, and the other part wanting to turn around, take Balder and ride hard for the north to wherever Zam and Lila were.

An hour later, they could see the edges of the small town, and the noises of people going about their lives floated on the air. They passed through a tiny market that had food, clothing, general goods, and at the far end, Maks could see the horses. He grimaced and made his feet keep walking.

The young woman who stood out the front of the corral eyed him and Jasten up, but her eyes lingered on Jasten, who totally ignored her.

She wore leather pants and a flowing dark yellow top that highlighted her light brown skin. Her hair was bound up in braids that showed off what looked like multiple colors no person was ever born with. Maks raised a brow. "We need a horse and . . . I have one I'd like you to care for. Not to resell."

Her gray eyes swept over to him. "You need board for a horse, we can do that. How long?"

Maks's jaw ticked. "Till the end of his life, or till I come back for him."

She blinked a few times. "That'll cost you."

Jasten grunted. "You can't be sure she wouldn't trade him out as a plow horse."

Batman grunted as if he'd been sucker punched, and though Maks knew the timing was coincidental, it still struck him.

That left only one option. "Two months. If I'm not back in two months, give him mercy."

The woman's eyes softened. "I will not trade him as a plow horse. You have my word." She lifted a hand to Batman who nuzzled her fingers, then pressed his head against her chest, for all the world like he was happy to come home. Or maybe he was happy to not have to run.

"My name is Ama."

Jasten turned. "I will pick up supplies while you finish here."

Maks took off Batman's gear, knowing this day would have come at some point. The saddle came off one last time, and once Batman was in a small paddock, he slid off his bridle. "Well done, my friend. Rest now. You've earned it."

He turned away and carried the gear out of the paddock. Then he went to Balder and touched his neck. "You pick out our new companion."

Balder bobbed his head, but first went to Batman. He reached across the fence and bunted his friend's nose with his own. Batman gave him a sideways nip and flipped his head at his friend as if to say get on with it.

The gray gelding gave a soft whinny, then turned and stepped out along the line of horses, smelling them, touching them with his nose and finally stopping beside the one at the far end. He whinnied again and Maks went to see the choice.

A big pair of brown eyes turned to look at him from under long dark lashes that were about as feminine as a horse could get. Her coat was a solid black, so dark that there were spots of color that reminded him of Zam's hair. She wasn't as heavily built as Batman, leaner than both him and Balder.

"You sure she can carry me?" He was no slouch in the weight department.

Ama came to stand next to him. "She came from the Plains of Despair. She will run like the wind for you. There is a cost, of course, for such a horse."

They haggled, but not for long, which should have made him nervous. The smile she flashed him should have made him nervous too. But Balder had picked the mare, so he trusted that she would work out.

He put the saddle on, and she hunched her back. He shot a look at Ama who grinned. "You never asked if she'd been ridden."

Maks beckoned for Balder to come closer. "You need to explain to your friend here that we need her to do as you do and be good. I don't have time to train a new horse and make it to Zam."

Balder snorted and put his nose against the nose of the new horse. He looked her over while he waited. "What do we call you?"

A clank of pots turned his head to see Jasten rejoin them at the paddocks. The shifter lifted his head. "Perhaps Queen, for is she not a beauty worthy of a queen?"

The mare gave a soft nicker and leaned into Balder, and Maks tentatively tightened up the girth. She didn't so much as flinch. Nor did she balk when he slid the bridle up over her ears and adjusted it for her head. So, apparently, she liked the name. He was taking careful note that this horse was not acting like a typical horse and his suspicions rose higher yet when he smoothed the hair back on her forehead.

A fresh wound, still scabbing and healing in the middle of her skull, made his heart skip a beat. So that was why Balder picked her.

"Good girl." He patted her neck and slipped her an oat ball.

Then without further questioning, he swung up into the saddle. Her back hunched again under him and she gave a couple hops across the ground like a crow testing things out, then settled under him.

He glanced at Ama. "Thanks. She'll be perfect."

With one last look at a now-sleeping Batman, he turned his new mount and led Balder to where Jasten stood waiting with supplies.

"We have enough to get us to the next settlement," his companion said. "You sure that mare is going to be good? She won't have any muscling from previous riding by the sound of things."

Maks nodded. "She'll be good. And she'll more than keep up with Balder."

They started at a walk, picked up to a trot and then he relaxed his hold on the reins and let the mare pick her own pace. She shot forward, bucking and dropping her head between her front feet in a last-ditch attempt to throw him off.

He clung to the saddle as the world bobbed up and down. Balder gave a sharp, trumpeting whinny, more like a stallion than the gelding he was.

The mare slowed and shook her head once, then settled into a ground-eating gallop that for the shock of Maks, Balder had to work to keep up to.

Maks leaned into the mare's neck and let the miles fly by as they raced south to find the ships, to find their way to Zam.

Hours passed before they began to slow, and Queen let Balder finally catch up to her. The horses were breathing hard, and so was Jasten. "Damn, they move like the wind."

As if on cue, a swirl of the desert went by in a tiny twister, and Maks followed it with his eyes.

A dust cloud that grew even as he watched. He pointed it out to Jasten. "Natural?"

Jasten shaded his eyes. "Looks like it. We get them all the time, sandstorms and the like."

They rode on, and Maks kept his eye half on the storm riding their right flank, almost as if . . . as if it were keeping pace.

"Jasten, you sure?" He pointed again at the cloud to their right.

Jasten shook his head. "Weird, but not unheard of," he shouted over the now-howling wind and the sound of the horses' hooves against the hard ground.

A bolt of lightning struck the desert right in front of them and the two horses slid to a stop, landing on their butts, they stopped so fast.

Maks jerked his reins to the right, away from the storm, and both Queen and Balder followed his lead. Another bolt of lightning, another and another until they were boxed in by it.

The sandstorm ripped around them, swirling faster and faster, blinding them as surely as the lightning had stopped them.

"You ride such pretty ponies," a voice called through the storm. "What makes you special enough to ride the hornless?"

Maks shaded his eyes, squinting them against the battering sand and finally closing them. "They are our friends."

"They are no one's friends!" The voice belonged to a woman, from what Maks could hear, but otherwise he had nothing on just who had found them and decided to make their day miserable.

The storm died as suddenly as it had started and ropes settled around his upper body, pinning his arms to his sides as he was yanked out of the saddle.

He hit the dirt hard, knocking the wind out of

him a big whoosh. His horse danced next to him. "Go, fly!" he yelled at her. "Balder, go! Get to Zam!" The two horses bolted away and the woman screamed.

"You son of a bitch!"

A boot hit him square in the back and he arched away from the blow too late. Pain radiated up and through his body in a way that told him that was no simple boot kick. There had been magic in it, directing it, spreading the pain through his limbs until he was limp with it.

"Gather them up," she barked and strode in front of him finally. Though his gaze was fogged with pain, he still saw her. Still saw the magic in her and recognized it as his own.

She was a Jinn.

And was seriously pissed.

"Stop this." He coughed and spit blood to the side. "We mean no harm. We've done nothing wrong."

"It is not a matter of wrong, slug. It is that you stole what is mine to take as I please. Those two hornless were mine, and you told them to fly. Now they are gone, and I have two measly new slaves to show for it." She kicked him again for good measure, once more stealing his breath.

Jasten was on the ground across from him, eyes closed, breathing labored. "Lady of the Storm, please . . . we mean no harm. As he says, we were only trying to get to Port Phantos."

"The Port of Phantos is not in your future," she cooed. "You are my slave now, shifter. And you, what are you?"

She grabbed Maks's face and jerked it upward. But the second her hand touched his skin she hissed and stepped back. "Jinn."

"As you are," he pointed out, not sure why she seemed so shocked. Her next words answered his unspoken question.

"There are no male Jinn alive past three days of age. So while you carry no power, that would not have mattered unless you were deliberately hidden," she said. "Where are you from?"

He had to school his face not to glare at her. In that moment, he was a small cub again, facing down a raging Marsum for some perceived wrong and he'd learned those lessons well on how to play the part. He lowered his eyes and let his body slump in defeat. "I came from Mamitu's holding." Not a lie.

The female Jinn jerked his face up once more so she could stare down into his eyes. "You are not lying, but neither are you telling me the whole truth. It seems that I might need to teach you the meaning of obedience."

Jasten groaned softly. "I should have died before this day came."

Maks turned his head as he was lifted to his feet, several large men to either side of him, dragging him by his bound arms toward a billowing cloud of dust.

"Tell yer bird to knock that shit off!" the eldest man said. He stood out from the others with his closely shorn gray hair and lines chiseled into his face from years of the sun and weather beating down on him.

The dust storm settled and what stood in the middle of it made Maks's legs wobble. The bird was as big as any dragon with a wingspan just as wide. Tawny feathers with black points on its head, tips of the wings and tail feathers made the bird that much more striking. Button-black eyes half the size of his own body swiveled to look at them. It clacked its beak, showing off tiny teeth inside.

On its back was a harness set up that allowed for half the men, including him and Jasten, to be strapped into the leather seating.

The female Jinn mounted a second bird, just as large, by herself, and waved a hand at the remaining men. "Get to the keep."

Without any other commands, the birds leapt into the sky, their ochre wings disappearing in a cloud of sand and dust that swirled up around them, filling his ears and working its way into every inch of his clothing. Maks closed his eyes and tried to think of a bright side to this.

The horses had escaped, that was good.

But loose, with tack on, they would be a target for any person out there looking for them.

Time ticked by and he tried to see where they were going, he did. But every time he opened his eyes the dust slammed into his eyeballs and he had to close them once more.

There was a sudden drop where his stomach lurched and someone behind him heaved.

"Keep that shit in!" the same older man hollered as the birds dropped again, and again, until they landed, hopping twice and then going still.

Maks was pulled off, and he struggled to see where they were.

On the coast, that much was certain, the ocean raging out in front of him. He turned and blinked. Not on the coast.

Somewhere in the middle of the ocean on an island.

The female Jinn strode in front of him, smirking. She paused and stared down at him, her eyes hard and unforgiving. "I see in you that you think to escape? That you think already there is a way for you to get back to the mainland? To your life?"

He lowered his gaze, faking submission, and did not answer her. He knew her type, she would just keep on talking.

She bent at the waist and grabbed his chin, jerking it up and forcing him to stare her in the eyes. "Welcome to the Sea of Storms, slave. Where no one takes a step without my permission."

Balder's father carried us to the edge of the plains by the end of the day. By the best calculations I had, we'd crossed close to two hundred miles. In eight hours. A trek that under normal circumstances would have taken us closer to a week, doing about thirty miles a day to save the horses, and my own ass.

Our timeline of three weeks was being condensed rapidly. The unicorn had saved us six days. Now as long as we didn't blow that lead all to shit, we'd be good.

"Holy shit." I slid from his back as the sun dipped low off to our left, and I helped a sleepy Reyhan down. The stallion grunted and trotted off, dropped his head and started grazing, chomping at the long grass with a vigor that reminded me of a teenage boy digging into his dinner as if he hadn't eaten for a week.

I took a step and wobbled, I'll admit it. Even with all my years riding, that eight hours at a speed I could barely believe, being held on by the stallion's magic, was hard on my limbs and ass.

Reyhan, on the other hand, bobbled about no problem, picking flowers and weaving them into the stallion's hair, giving him a splash of purple, pink and yellow. He snorted and then lay down so she could put the flowers through his tail too while he continued to eat in a circle around his upper body.

"Vain." I pointed a finger at him and he lifted his upper lip, flapping it up and down as he showed off his teeth to me, making Reyhan giggle.

Yeah, he was smitten with the girl.

Every time she got close to his face, he ruffled her hair with his lips, making her laugh all that much harder, the sound of her joy filling the air and easing some of the stress sitting on my shoulders.

I couldn't fault him for being so taken by her. She was sweet and cute as a button, and on top of that, had a good head on her shoulders. Despite the trauma she'd been through, she'd kept it together and helped me survive the rabisu bites. I wasn't sure that just any five- or six-year-old could manage to do so.

Lila flew around me in circles, fresh as the flowers that Reyhan was picking. "I could never have covered that distance without having my bigger shape back."

"Balder couldn't have covered that distance in that time," I said softly, missing my boy. Hoping he was safe.

I lay back in the grass and stared at the slowly darkening sky, the dredges of sunlight still kissing the colors of the world in places. "Lila, I don't think the river will be far. We can ride the edge of it until we find the rock that looks like wings."

"Yes. But there is that Nasnas monster that Steve told us about." Lila grimaced. "Goddess of the desert, I hate even saying his name! I thought when Steve number one had died, we were done with him."

I sat up with a grimace. "You and me both." I reached up and touched the now-scabbed wounds on the back of my neck. "The touch of the Nasnas monster eats flesh, so, like your acid maybe? We have to come up with a way to kill it from a distance." I pulled my sword from my back, the whispers of death in my head easily ignored. "This will bring me too close. A bow and arrow would be better."

In my hands the blade shivered, morphing in front of my eyes into a solid length of a bow, right down to the tautly pulled string. I held it up. "Seriously?"

*I bring death in any way you wish.*

That was the most cognizant sentence the blade had whispered, and of course, she went silent after that. Which was fine.

"So you have a bow now." Lila leapt up into the sky. "Let me see if I can find some arrows."

I sat there with this new weapon in my hand and wondered if someone was playing a trick on me. I gripped the weapon, stood and pulled it to my cheek. I let the string fly and it smacked my hand gripping the bow.

"Fuck!" I yelped and danced about, shaking my hand. That smarted. I turned to see Reyhan with her hands over her ears. "Sorry."

"My dad says that's a dirty word that ladies should never use." She lowered her hands.

"I'm not a lady, so it's okay," I said. Gah, I'd make a terrible parent. "But he's right. If you're a lady, you shouldn't use it." There, that would help. Like a footnote in a contract. Barely noticed by anyone unless you were in trouble.

She frowned. "Maybe I don't want to be a lady then. You are strong, and you fight good. I'd rather be able to fight good."

I held up a hand, stopping her. "Look, until you are older, you can't use that word. Okay?"

She turned back to braiding flowers into the stallion's mane. "He needs a name, you know."

I sighed. "He likely has one, and just isn't telling us yet. He will when he is ready."

Walking over to them, I sat on the other side of the white stallion and leaned against his side, pressing my cheek to his hide. He even smelled like Balder, the scent of horse and hay, and a bit of something else, like the sweet smell of a flower that was only here, in his coat.

I slid an arm around him and found myself drifting between consciousness and sleep. This was no ordinary slumber. I could feel the yank on my awareness, and at first, I fought it until I realized it was him, the stallion. Apparently he wanted to talk.

*The weapon you carry is dangerous.*

His big dark eyes swept over and somehow through me. I blinked and took a slow breath. I sat in front of him while he lay on the ground.

"All weapons are dangerous," I mumbled.

*That one will steal you away. You must be careful, little cat.* A pause. *You and your companions may call me by my name given at birth, an honor I do not give to any outside my herd. Torin.*

"Good name," I whispered. "I like it. Thank you."

He grunted and I opened my eyes to a tugging on my hands and Reyhan in my face. "I'm hungry."

I nodded and pushed up to my feet, pulled a few sticks and piled a little grass to make a fire.

Lila was not back yet, but I wasn't too worried. The connection between us was strong, and if something had gone wrong while she was scouting about, I was sure I'd know. I lit the fire and fed it fuel as it got going more, pushing back the dark.

From my pack, I brought out the bit of food we had and gave a little to Reyhan. "Stay here, I'll hunt up some more food. Tell Lila where I've gone, okay? And do not go anywhere. Stay with Torin."

She mumbled an okay around a mouthful of food and I turned, shifting into my jungle cat form. Loping away through the long grass, I scented for the jackrabbits I'd seen bounding away from Torin's hooves.

Catching a whiff of them, I lowered myself to my belly and slunk forward, slowly stalking the prey that were just this side of too big for my smaller house cat form.

Two jackrabbits were on top of each other. Fucking rabbits.

I leapt forward and killed them both with one bite, snapping their heads off. Two rabbits this size was plenty for the three of us. I shifted once more to two legs, bent and scooped up the rabbits and headed back to the fire. A quick skinning, and we'd be eating good for the night and the morning. Full bellies were a good way to push back any fear.

I looked up as I drew close to the fire, words tugging on my ears from a voice I did not know.

No unicorn lay near the fire.

No Reyhan sat braiding his hair with flowers.

I dropped the rabbits and reached for my blade, only it was a bow. Damn it.

The bow morphed in my hands, turning back into the short sword.

*They did kill your companions, take their heads quickly!*

The words cut into my brain and I was moving before I thought better of it, as if my body was not my own. I wanted to stop, to go in slowly, not rush to kill whoever was there! Fuck, this was what I'd been warned of.

Like another person was holding the strings to my limbs, I kept moving. I kept my sword arm up, ready to hack off a head even though I was trying to make my arm drop. Trying to make my body obey me.

"Fuck you!" I growled, taking hold of one small part of my limbs. My thumb. I popped it open and the blade dropped to the ground. I stumbled to a stop. Maybe this was worse than the flail.

I left the weapon there on the ground and pulled my two smaller knives, one from the top of my boot, the other from my hip.

They would do just fine and they didn't try to force my hand in the most literal of senses. I crept closer and the voice became clearer.

"Hello? I'm lost. Can you help me?"

I didn't see anyone, and it took me a minute to pinpoint where exactly the voice was coming from.

I stood and stared down at the small dragon curled up near the fire. Scales of brilliant red and gold flashed against the fire light. His big blue eyes shot to mine, then to my knives. He scuttled back, his butt right in the flames but he didn't seem to be overly bothered. "Please, don't hurt me."

I lowered my weapons, tucking them away. "I won't hurt you, but . . . where did you come from? How did you get here?"

He peered at me around the fire. I looked out into the semi-darkness and spotted Torin's hide easily. He'd taken Reyhan out of harm's way. I motioned for the two of them to come closer. Lila was going to shit her scales when she saw this one. Was he a baby hatchling? Or was he like her, somehow caught in a shape that was too small for the dragon world?

He limped around the fire. "I escaped from Asag. They didn't want me. I'm too little."

Little he was, maybe even a bit smaller than Lila.

Lila dropped out of the sky and landed right in front of him. "Holy Winchester Goose! He's no bigger than me!"

She shot forward and he belched fire at her. She screeched and flipped to the side. "You shit, why would you do that?"

I looked at Torin who shook his head once. Reyhan sat on his back, her eyes wide. I had a feeling that before this journey was over, she would have permanently widened them.

The small red dragon gave a low hiss. "The lady said she would not hurt me!"

"She's no lady," Reyhan offered. "She says fuck."

I could have died right there, but as it was, I burst out laughing. "The child is correct. I am no lady, but I always keep my word. No harm will come to you as long as you bring no harm to us."

He scrambled across the ground and that was when I saw he had no wings. I bent and offered him my hand and he wrapped himself around my forearm. He might have only seemed smaller because there were no wings to give him more size. He clung to me, shivering. "You smell like blood."

I sighed, feeling his claws hook into me. "Lila, there are two rabbits just beyond there." I pointed back the way I'd come. "Would you mind? And avoid the sword; it's being a shit."

She flew past us and gave the red dragon a look I couldn't decipher. I went to the fire and lowered the little guy to the ground. "Warm up, we'll get some food into you. You like innards?"

His mouth hung open and a droplet of fire leaked out and onto the ground with a hiss. "Yes."

"Use your manners," Reyhan said. "Please and thank you, and 'scuse me when you fart or burp."

Torin lay down once more. She slid from his side and went and scooped up the little dragon, holding him tightly to her chest as she sat by the fire.

He leaned into her and sighed, closing his eyes. Yes, Reyhan definitely had a knack with the animals.

Lila brought me the rabbits without a word, which I skinned and gutted quickly. She left all the innards to our new friend, and I left her a rabbit to herself. They were big enough for me and Reyhan to share one and have leftovers in the morning even splitting things with an extra mouth.

The smell of cooking meat curled up through the night air.

"My name is Castor," the red dragon said softly

after he'd finished eating and before we could ask. "I hatched about twenty years ago, and they waited to see if I would grow." He shrugged and curled tighter around himself. "Never happened."

Lila crept closer and tapped a claw on his back. "Did you have wings?"

"They cut them off. They cut off the wings of any dragon they deem useless," he whispered.

Lila let out a rumbling snarl. "There is no such thing as a useless dragon."

I leaned back, finding Torin, letting Lila take the lead here with the newcomer. She would know far better what to ask, and how to ask it. She paced in front of Castor, peppering him with questions.

How many dragons were there?

How were they kept there, the ones that still had wings?

What were they being used for?

How many hatchlings were there right then?

How many eggs?

"Slow down, please," he said, his body trembling. "I can answer some of this but not all. They kept those of us they considered useless far away from the rest. As if we were contagious." He paused and sighed. "But I know there were a thousand dragons that they were using, at least. And I saw a cart of eggs brought in before I was kicked out. Maybe another two dozen eggs?"

Lila looked at me, then at Castor. "Why do they keep stealing the eggs? Are they not breeding their own now?"

Oh, that was a good question, and one I hadn't considered.

Castor shook his head. "None are fertile. They don't know if it's because the eggs are jostled when they are stolen, or because of some other factor, but they can't reproduce. So they must always take more eggs."

"And where did you plan on going?" I asked. "Out across this wide world on rather small legs, if you don't mind me saying so."

He blinked a few times. "There is something calling me to the west, and rumors of a land filled with free dragons. Dragons that answer to no one but their king and queen." He sighed. "I want to go to them, to ask them why they haven't come for us. We know we are stolen, we can still remember our mothers' voices from when we were in the shells. We can still hear their anger and pain as we were taken from them. Why did they not come for us?"

His jaw ticked and he looked away. Lila crept up into Reyhan's arms and curled around the other dragon.

"The mothers were forbidden," Lila said softly. "The fathers were sent to find the missing eggs, and when they came back they said that the eggs had all been taken into the east, to where there was no return. We all thought that meant they'd been killed or eaten."

His big blue eyes closed, and she squeezed around him tighter. "You are not alone now, Castor. And we are going to save the hatchlings. We are going to stop this theft once and for all."

The next morning dawned cool and misty, the ground wet with dew on the blades of grass around us. Lila and Castor were curled together near the dying embers. She'd not once slept next to me the night before. I understood, and yet I could see that this was the start of something for her that even Trick couldn't give her.

A soul that understood exactly what she'd lived through. Even if he was just a friend, he was a friend who understood even more than I did.

I stood and turned to find Torin waiting patiently. I scooped up Reyhan in my arms and the last of the rabbit meat and set her on Torin's back first. Then I scooped up the sleeping dragons and set them in her arms. "You hold them tight. We're going to go fast again."

The two dragons had talked late into the night when they thought the rest of us slept.

I went to where the sword lay on the ground away from our group, and pushed it with my toe. "If you're not going to behave, I'll bury you right here and let you rust."

*Fine.*

I bent and scooped up the sword, putting it into its scabbard without hurrying, but also not dawdling. There was no feel to it, yet now that I knew it could take hold of me, I wasn't so quick to want to pull it free again. I grabbed my bedroll, checked the shotgun to make sure it was tied on tightly, and then went to the others.

"We're ready," I said as I leapt up onto Torin's back.

His innate magic wrapped around us once more, locking us in place onto his back. The stallion went from a standstill into a gallop with only a couple strides as he bore us off the plains and into the shadows of a mountain with a broken peak.

I stared at the top, seeing it again in my mind when Mamitu had shown me the way to the Vessel of Vahab.

"Veer to the left." I pointed at the glimmering

snake of a river. "Keep your distance from the water but follow it."

Torin gave a quick snort and changed direction with a flick of his hooves. We reached the river and stayed thirty feet off the bank, which was still close enough to see the sleek scaled bodies under the clear running water, thirty and forty feet long. There was no hiding them. Beady eyes broke the surface and long snouts snapped water in our direction. Snouts full of teeth.

The long bodies had two clawed legs up front, but the back end morphed into a powerful fishtail that propelled them alongside us longer than I liked before they fell back and another took their place.

Torin flicked his head which caught the light on his horn. "Yeah," I said, "I'd like to run them through too, but only if they get close. So let's steer clear as best we can."

The hours ticked by as we followed the river. We were moving almost as fast as we had the day before, and I kept my eyes peeled to the landscape as we raced along.

I wanted to talk to Lila, to ask her thoughts, or maybe even just swap Shakespeare with her. But she slept on and it wasn't long until Reyhan joined her, the lull of Torin's pace drawing her back to sleep.

I wished Maks were with us. Even knowing he couldn't be I had a moment of pure longing, and for a split second, I turned my head, staring to the south. As if . . . I closed my eyes and saw behind the lids a wall of water, an island and Maks. There and gone as I opened my eyes, wondering if I'd somehow fallen asleep along with Reyhan.

But my head was still turned and I felt that pull to the south. Toward Maks. My heart clipped up a notch. Call me suspicious, but what if he was in trouble? This side of the desert was full of unknowns, as I'd already found out. What if one of those unknowns had tackled him to the ground? Or to the water as the case might be.

Jaw ticking, I forced my eyes away from the south and the sensation of Maks. If he was in trouble, I'd find him. I'd get him out. That was the deal. We saved one another.

Suddenly the feeling of having bought myself time slid away. We'd bought time, but was it enough to get Maks once we had the Vessel of Vahab?

We rounded another curve in the bank of the river, and with those few strides, the shadow of the mountain began to loom over us. I looked ahead, seeing the river go on for miles before it disappeared into the mountains.

But that wasn't what made my heart falter. No,

the rock that was shaped like a pair of wings was ahead of us, at the base of the mountain as the river split in two directions.

I patted Torin's neck. "Ease up, we're close."

He slowed to a trot and then to a walk, blowing air hard and clearing his lungs. I slid off his back first and Lila finally woke up. She yawned and stretched. "Wow, I was sound asleep."

I nodded. "That's what you get for talking all night."

"Not all night," she said. "We were asleep by the time the sun was breaking overhead." She grinned and flew by me, her smile saying it all.

Smitten.

Goddess almighty, a smitten dragon was fine under any other circumstance, but I needed her focus today of all days. "Lila, we're here. Keep an eye out for the Nasnas monster. I want to look about and see if there is any better way to get past it."

I didn't have a frame of reference for this new monster, other than it was probably aquatic. Which really didn't give me a lot of confidence after seeing the reptilian creatures that had paced us and were even now following along the river. At least they wouldn't be coming out of the water with those fishtails. I hoped.

I put a hand against Torin's neck. "I need to

find a place for Reyhan to stay out of the fight. You and Castor can stick close to her."

His dark eyes blinked at me like he thought I was being a fool, but he jogged away from the river, putting more distance between them and the most likely place for the battle.

"Here." Lila dropped a few arrows at my feet. "There are a bunch of them up there near the Y in the river."

I scooped the arrows up and stared at them, recognizing the language and the style, shocked at what I was seeing. "These belong to gorcs. Could one of the Jinn masters have sent an army in?"

Mamitu had said the armies had been big, powerful, and they'd all failed.

I did a slow turn, suddenly wondering if we were about to be ambushed by the creations belonging to the Jinn, creations that hated shifters. Sure, they had gone rogue and started breeding on their own, and they'd become more numerous, and in theory they shouldn't be here. Which begged the question, why were there arrows from a gorc troop so far east?

I rolled them in my hands. Six arrows tipped with iron, the fletchings still intact. "Either they aren't from all that long ago, or they are preserved somehow." I ran my hands over each arrow, feeling for something, anything that would give a clue as to just how this could be. Also I was stalling.

Because a troop of determined gorcs was no small thing.

"Looks like there were fifty of them." Lila landed on my shoulder. "So lots of arrows. But no armor that I can see, and no footprints."

"Only the arrows didn't work," I said softly. I didn't know what the answer was to this riddle, and I was sure it was a riddle. "The Nasnas monster guards the Vessel of Vahab, and the reptilian creatures monitor the river. What do you want to bet that even if we kill the Nasnas monster, we'll open up new territory for them?"

Lila groaned. "What are you thinking?"

I paced up and down the river, still far enough away that we weren't targets, and not all that near to the winged rock. For the moment, we were in neutral territory.

"I'm not thinking of anything right now, just waiting for the answer to come to me," I said as I paced and rolled the arrows in my hands. Movement on the far side of the bank caught my eye. A deer and a couple rabbits stepped out toward the water. The rabbits went first, hopping forward, stealing a drink and then bounding away. The deer was slower, eyes and ears flicking this way and that. A small set of antlers spread wide off the top of its head. Young then, and too stupid to realize what a bad idea drinking from the river could be, even if the rabbits had done it without harm.

Lila landed on my shoulder to watch with me. We both knew what was coming, but the how of it might be helpful with what we were facing.

The young buck almost slunk to the water's edge and lowered its head to drink. A few gulps and it was backing away, moving fast.

Not fast enough.

The jaws of a croc swept up and out as its fish-tail propelled it farther out of the water than I wanted to believe possible, at least twenty-five feet up the bank. Its jaws closed on the back end of the deer and yanked it into the water as quick as a striking desert snake.

Even from where we were, the blood could be seen on the water.

I waited, not moving an inch as the water rumbled and stirred around the kill. That wasn't what had my attention, though. Upstream some-thing stirred, something bigger even than the croc-odiles. The river water sloshed and the croc grabbed its kill and swam away, downriver before the much bigger monster made a grab for its food.

The whole scene played out in a matter of two, three minutes tops, which I took careful note of.

Slowly, a plan began to form. I backed farther from the river, wanting more than the forty feet we had between us and the water's edge. Even though my plan was giving me the heebie-jeebies, I started to speak.

"The Nasnas monster has to eat, yes? What if we killed a couple of the beasties with the big mouths and fishtails? The scent of blood will bring the Nasnas downriver. Like with the rabisu, I'll take my house cat form. Stay small. The monsters ignored the rabbits. We stay low and while the Nasnas monster feeds, I'll go for a sprint upstream and then a quick swim."

Her claws tightened on my shoulder hard enough she was going to leave dents. "I don't know. In theory it sounds good, but that's how plans go. They sound good but often don't work. So what's the backup plan?"

I licked my lips. "You drop some acid on the Nasnas and keep its eyes facing south. Keep it as distracted as you can from what I'm doing."

She grunted. "Okay. I say we go in here." She pointed at the river just ahead of us. "Well before the Y and where the vessel is buried under sand and water—you remember that part, don't you?"

I nodded. "I do. I'll shift to my jungle cat shape once I'm at the bottom. Big paws, big diggers."

"Poo diggers," she muttered and I laughed.

"Lila, if you have a different plan, speak now or forever hold your peace." I stripped off my cloak and boots, and my hip bag. I left the one weapon on my back that whispered death to me, and pulled the more modern one free of my bedroll. I put the pieces of the shotgun together and put a grenade in the launcher. Then I forced myself to get within range of the snapping teeth. Forty feet, thirty-five, thirty, twenty-five, twenty.

"Close enough!" Lila whispered.

"This will make a lot of noise and draw a lot of attention to this end of the river," I said as I strode forward another five feet. I could see three of the crocs right there, and their eyes were slowly turning my way. "Let's hope it's enough to give us the time we need."

I swallowed, lifted the shotgun and aimed at the eyes of the reptilian creature closest to the edge. I squeezed the trigger and the gun went off. The creature rolled in the water, a red bloom filling the area around him.

Another came closer and I shot it too, then reloaded. "Lila, watch for movement upriver."

"Nothing yet," she said.

I fired on two more, taking them with first shots. A group swam toward the now nicely chummed water and I flicked the gun to the under-barrel grenade launcher and fired into the group.

The thump of the gun, the explosion of water and bits of pieces of flesh ...

"Oh, we got something," Lila said. "The water is coming fast, rippling like a wave! Way faster than before!"

I fired another grenade into a second group of reptiles, threw the gun back out to where my cloak and bedroll were, and shifted to my house cat form. "Going!"

I slid down to four small feet and raced upriver, using the rocks and clumps of river marsh to hide my passage. The wave of water went by me, soaking my paws, but not slowing me for a second. I leapt over what I thought was a log, then saw it for what it was—the bones of a gorc, or partial bones of a gorc—but didn't slow.

The thrashing of water behind me was a good sign.

I chose to think so, anyway.

"Keep going!" Lila yelled, pacing me. "They are fighting over the food!"

The Y was just ahead of me and I forced myself back to two legs with only a small stumble. Lila shot ahead and I motioned for her to get away.

"Here, directly at the split. I can see a glimmer of

something!" she shouted, and then she flew back downriver to hold her position. I bolted along, took a breath and dove into the water, swimming for all I was worth, suddenly grateful again for the Oasis and the time I'd spent there as a child, learning to swim.

At the split, I treaded water and looked down at my feet, the water pulling me in two directions. The glimmer Lila had seen was there, a glitter of gold. I took a breath and went down, under the surface, arms and legs kicking hard, driving me to the bed of the river. There, I shifted again to my jungle cat form and used my big paws to dig away the sand rapidly.

My lungs and muscles did not like all the movement, all the running and swimming and now the deprivation of air. I wasn't going to be able to do this in one shot like I'd hoped. I turned and swam for the surface, gasped a breath of air and then was pushed under by a wave of water.

I forced my head up, got another gulp and went back under, making it to the bottom as a dark shape blocked out the light around me.

Not good, not good, not good. The refrain rippled through me as I dug around the golden . . . box. It was a box. How the hell was I going to get this up?

I wasn't. I had to open it now.

One more shift, back to two legs, and I had to

go up again for air. I rolled and stared up at the belly of the creature that was above me. Not in the water but hovering over it and standing on what looked like hundreds of spindly jelly legs. I swam up as quietly as I could, broke the surface and stayed there, breathing quietly, gaining the air and respite I needed.

"Come on, you giant ugly water bug!" Lila screamed from somewhere up high, but the creature didn't move.

I didn't dare tell her that I was okay. Because that would be a lie. I was okay, at the moment, but the second I had to get out of the water, I was screwed. The pull of the river made me hesitate and an idea bloomed.

Lila wouldn't like it, but hell, she didn't like most of my plans so what was one more added to the list? It would work. I was mostly sure of it.

One last big gulp of air and I went down under the surface, straight to the bottom. I pulled a knife and worked it around the edge of the box, popping the seal. A rumble above me told me my time was up.

The lid was open, the bottom of the river stirring up with silt as the monster's hundreds of legs trampled around me, and I reached in blindly for the vessel that should be there. My fingers curled around the handle and I jerked it out as the

Nasnas monster realized its treasure was about to be stolen. I pushed off the bottom, not toward the surface, but with the pull of the current that drew toward the mountains.

All I could hope was that the crocs were only on one side of the river. Yeah, that thought hit me a little too late.

I rolled and pulled Lilith from my back as I shot toward the jelly legs that were acid to the touch. Anything the flesh of the Nasnas touched would be incinerated, melted into nothing. I really didn't want to deal with that shit.

If anything could cut through them and keep my hide intact, it would be the sister weapon to my flail.

I swung, tucked and rolled through the open space that had been legs only a moment before. One brushed against my upper thigh and I couldn't help the scream of bubbles that escaped me. With a golden vessel in one hand and my blade in the other, it was all I could do to kick to the surface and encourage the river to sweep me away.

I popped up, and Lila was on me in a flash. "What are you doing?"

I shifted into my house cat form and she grabbed me, yanking me out of the river as a jelly leg slammed where I'd been only a moment before.

"Just going for a swim!" I yelled back as she swept us away from the river and a roaring Nasnas monster. The whole thing looked like it was jelly from its legs to its bulbous body and head that rolled and vibrated with anger, right to every single leg.

"That thing is awful!" Lila said. "You should have seen how it tore the crocodile things apart! Like they were made of paper."

Even as she spoke, I could feel the afterburn of the acid. "I was lucky. I only got a little on my leg."

She squeaked and flew to the ground, rolling me over to inspect the wound. "You're right, maybe because you were under the water it's not as bad. It's not eating through."

The sound of hoofbeats and I turned as Torin trotted up to us. Reyhan held Castor around the middle, his body flopping on either side of her arms like he'd like to get away but couldn't without hurting her, and he wasn't going to do that.

I pulled myself onto Torin's back, pulled a sack from my bedroll and stuffed the Vessel of Vahab into it, then to be safe tied it to Torin's mane. "We have bought time with Torin's speed. But we have to go further south before we take this back to Mamitu."

Lila gripped me hard. "What is to the south? Oh, crap, Toad is in trouble, isn't he?"

I nodded. "Yeah, he is. And he needs rescuing."

I held the Vessel of Vahab tightly in one hand, my other arm around Reyhan.

We had to make it in time. We had to.

The Sea of Storms circled a large island that the aptly named Storm Queen held as her keep. There was no way Maks could see exactly how big the island was, but he knew one thing for sure. Even if he escaped the bonds that held him, and he was released, there would be no way to swim back to the mainland.

He would need to borrow one of her birds.

Or find himself a dragon.

In that moment, he had never missed Lila and her bigger frame so much. He bowed his head, the weight of what he was facing sinking into him in a wave of despair.

They had been taken from the beach up to the keep made of dark gray stone, the rocks hard and cold under his knees, his hands tied behind his back, fingers numb from the hard knots.

The Storm Queen stopped in front of him, her tiny feet covered in simple black leather boots. "What is your name, new slave of mine?"

"Here lies a wretched corpse, of wretched soul bereft; seek not my name," he said softly, quoting Shakespeare. Wondering if she would even understand what it was he was saying. He wondered if she even knew the bard's words.

Her magic flared around him in a bright pulse of blue and green that drove into him suddenly, so hard that it arced him onto his toes and had him gasping for breath. Yeah, apparently, she knew exactly what he was saying, even if she didn't know Shakespeare.

"You would sass me? Let us make very sure that you learn your place." She snapped her fingers. The magic fled, and a rather large man who stood easily a head taller than Maks and had muscles on muscles was there. His arms were bare, and he wore a leather vest with a symbol of a crescent moon on fire etched into the middle of it. The giant of a man wore a hood, so there was no face to see any emotions on, like an executioner, and for one moment, Maks thought he was going to be killed.

Zam would not be happy if he got himself killed after she left him behind to save him.

Only it was far worse than that. He was grabbed by the throat and thrown across the courtyard, hands still bound. His body tumbled over and over and again he closed his eyes. This was not new to him, not really. He'd been at the hands of tormentors before. From that past experience, he knew he was in for a world of hurt.

He was picked up and dragged backward, his heels against the stone of the keep. Maks kept his body limp, knowing the minute he acted awake he'd be forced to walk, and right then he needed to save every ounce of energy and strength he had. Let the brute carry him, let him do the lion's share of the work.

"Rale, take him to the pits," the Storm Queen said. "I would have his name by nightfall, then in my bed shortly after."

*That* jerked Maks's head up and he stared at her as she smiled at him. "What? Do you think I would put you in the fields? That I would offer you a place fishing on my boats? The blood of a Jinn is uncommon, and a child of our union would be stronger than any other."

"I have a mate," he breathed out. "I will not touch you."

Her smile widened. "And where is your mate? This precious woman of yours? If she is a Jinn, she can challenge me for you." She stood in front of him. "Any Jinn worth her salt would not have allowed you to run free. Goddess only knows what damage a man can do on his own with no proper direction." Her smile widened as he clamped his jaw tightly, knowing that she was baiting him at best, and digging for information at the worst. If he said anything of Zam's journey, it would endanger her. This Storm Queen did not need to know anything about Zam.

She stepped closer to him, the leather she wore creaking, the smell of sweat and sea salt filling his nose. "You do not seem to understand that there will be no leaving this place. There will be no trace of where you have gone." Her hand reached up and cupped his chin, tipping his face to the side, inspecting him. "You will be a strong bloodline for my child, a daughter to become the next Storm Queen. And once I have what I want, then and only then will I let you die."

She stalked away from him, snapping her fingers. "I want one of the hornless, and if that means I need to do the task myself, so be it. Send my rhuk to the Plains of Despair and bring me the stallion."

Maks stared after her. She was going to take a

unicorn and cut its horn off? "Why?" The one-word question burst out of him.

She paused and stared back at him. "Give me your name, and I'll tell you."

Names had power and they both knew it. So perhaps it shocked her more than anything that he did.

"Maks."

Her eyebrows shot up as she strode toward him. "Maks, that's a good name. I like it. A unicorn that is not horned will be the mount of the one to take down Asag. I am that one. I am the grand-daughter of the Emperor, and the true ruler of the east."

And just like that, Maks knew he was more than a little in trouble. He was in shit so deep, he was going to drown before Zam found him.

Torin galloped back the way we'd come, along the side of the river, across the plains where his herd of unicorns acknowledged him with a chorus of whinnies, and there I slowed him with a touch of my hand. We'd ridden for over twelve hours to bring us to that point, at his breakneck speed that was both wonderous and painful to my backside.

I put more pressure into my touch, slowing him further.

"The rabisu wait on the other side of the slope. They gave us safe passage, but not you, Torin." I made a move to get off his back and he gave a small buck, keeping me in place. I slid off anyway. "At the very least, let's wait till morning. That is the smart move. Everyone can rest, you especially."

I poked a finger into his shoulder, and he flipped his lips at me, lowered his head and began to eat. Reyhan slept in my arms, snoring ever so slightly which made me smile. I laid her down and got my bedroll, setting it up for her, then wrapped her in it. She snuggled down and Castor joined her.

I walked away from them, stretching my legs, feeling . . . anxious. That was the only word for it. The sky was clear above us but for a few floating white clouds so thin as to barely be called clouds.

A crescent moon slit the sky and I stared at it, thinking about the pillars we'd run into earlier. Part of the rock army that belonged to Asag, the demon ruler. I frowned and kept staring up at the sky, looking for an answer there. Wishing I could ask for help from someone who knew more than I. Maybe even Mamitu. I'd take her advice even though I barely knew her.

And then a thought struck me.

Steve knew a lot.

He'd sworn he wouldn't kill me.

I worried at my bottom lip, thinking. Did I dare talk to him? Ask him questions again? Hope that he wasn't full of shit like the other Steve and would actually keep his word?

It was a chance I had to take. I was going to throw the rules out the window to go after Maks.

I took a few steps, then a few more toward the southern edge of the jungle. I made my way up the slope and stood at the top. "Steve-O, you want to have a chat?"

A series of chirps blew through the air and I tensed as the bushes ahead of me rustled, and then Steve stepped out onto the open ledge that looked out over the plains.

"You are back so soon?" He laced his fingers together and stared hard at me. "Or did you give up?"

"I had a fast ride." I tipped my head back toward the herd sleeping and grazing below. "But I have a question for you, and seeing as we're friends now, I'm hoping you will be able to answer me."

His face lifted, and if he'd had discernable eyebrows, I was sure they would have risen. "Tell me this question of yours." He gave a heavy pause. "Friend."

I pointed past him. "What lies to the farthest south of the land besides the ocean? Any monsters to speak of?"

Steve didn't move. "The south is dangerous, as is the east. But a different kind of danger. The Storm Queen resides there."

Now I had eyebrows and they shot up. "I thought the stories of a Storm Queen were just that. Stories."

He waved his hand at me. "Stories, even the most fanciful, come from somewhere. There are grains of truth in them all. The Storm Queen is dangerous as has every queen before her been. They bear one child—a daughter—and they are raised to be as deadly as the one before."

That was not part of the story I knew. The Storm Queen had power over weather more than anything else, and her fickle ways were the crux of many a story.

The sound of Lila flying close prepped me for her landing on my shoulder without jumping. She bobbed her head. "I don't know of this Storm Queen, and why are we talking about her?"

"She is in the south," I said. "And . . . I think that is where Maks is, so we need to be ready to avoid her." I said the words and they felt true. Maks was in the south, so that's where we were going.

Steve snorted. "Then he is as good as dead. Unless he ends up in her bed. She is of an age that she might be looking for a strong mate to produce her heir. Has he any abilities?"

Lila squeaked. "Jinn master."

Steve took a step back. "He is a . . . male Jinn? Then she will surely take him. That would give her the best chance at producing an heir of great power."

Well, fuck.

The urge to go now, to start toward the south, rose in me and I tamped it down. If the worst thing that happened to Maks was that he got bedded by a power-hungry woman, then he wasn't dead. I could deal with anything but dead.

I forced the bile and jealousy that stirred in my belly. "So you're saying he'll be flat on his back while we fight to get to him? Taking it leisurely like?"

The rabisu's eyes swept over me. "Does it not bother you—"

"OF COURSE, IT DOES BUT I CAN DO NOTHING ABOUT IT!" I may have yelled the words at him. Maybe.

Steve bowed his head. "You have passage through the jungle, but do not forget that you are the one the prophecy speaks of, and that in killing Asag, you free us all. Going after your mate . . . the saving of one may condemn hundreds of thousands to death, and slavery." He bowed at the waist.

I took a step back, hating that there might be even a kernel of truth in his words. "You have my gratitude for speaking to me of this." Very formal. Just like him.

I made my way down the slope and back to where Torin and the other unicorns stood. Not eating. Putting my hand on his hip, I felt him tense and then relax. "You should be eating."

He tipped his nose to the sky toward a growing bunch of clouds that seemed to be swirling up from the south.

Not one unicorn in the mixed herd so much as moved as the clouds spun closer to us, moving rapidly in a formation that I'd never seen before. "That is not natural. What the hell is it?"

Lila shot up into the air. "I'll get a closer look."

"Wait!" I said, but I was too slow. She was gone in a burst of speed, heading straight for the clouds that I was pretty sure were not clouds. My skin tickled and I knew in my belly that whatever was in those clouds was driven by magic. The closer they got, the more the magic felt . . . like mine.

I frowned. The wild magic I had inside of me had a taste all its own, and these clouds as they slid over the plains toward us came on a whisper of that same magic. But how was that possible? I had not made these clouds. I had no magic . . . unless what had been stolen from me was being used against us.

"Sweet baby goddess," I whispered. "That's my magic."

Torin turned his head and fixed me with his eye. There was no image with his look, but a feeling that burned through me.

*Not you.*

I tapped his hip and spoke my thoughts. "I know, but it's something like mine, and maybe my magic that was stolen is being used against us. That would be bad. We need to go."

As I spoke, Lila dive bombed. "Birds, giant birds big enough to pack away any of us!"

She spoke and the clouds cleared, revealing exactly what she'd said she saw. Birds as big as dragons with tawny feathers, points of their bodies tipped in black and talons large enough to easily encompass a unicorn or two.

"We need cover!" I yelled, already knowing the danger was on all sides. "Get to the jungle!"

Torin reared up and whinnied—sharp as a bugle blast that split the silence of the night.

I ran and scooped up a startled Reyhan and ran with her toward the slope that led up into the jungle. I had to get there first. I had to beg Steve to let the unicorns through.

I scrambled up ahead of the first of the unicorns, though barely.

Steve stood there, staring at me, and then at the unicorns.

"Hey, Steve. How's it hanging?" I asked as I set Reyhan down, keeping her hand in mine.

Steve's eyes lit hungrily on the colt's dark brown hide. "You bring a unicorn to my jungle? I cannot give him safe passage; his blood burns too bright, too hot for me to hold my children back."

I stared hard at him. "Don't be a Steve, Steve. You gave us safe passage. You want me to kill Asag? Then you need to let them through. Unharmed."

Behind us, the scream of the birds cut through the air, a booming shriek that made the unicorns shudder and bounce where they stood. They knew they couldn't just bolt into the jungle.

His eyes closed and when they opened, I knew I was in very deep shit. Shit up to my neck.

Orange eyes stared back at me. Not Steve's eyes, but eyes that I suspected belonged to one very bad demon. And I was sure enough, the voice was no longer Steve's. "You think you would kill me?"

I narrowed my eyes at him and made sure his eyes stayed on me. "I hear you're the biggest dick of them all. And you've been swinging it around, making people dance to your tune for years."

"You fell under the rabisu's spell once. I'm quite sure I can make him do it again." Steve—or maybe Asag—smirked at me and I flashed my teeth at him.

"Why is it with you, it's always talk, talk, talk, and nothing to back it up?" I adjusted my grip on Reyhan and whispered in her ear. "I need you to shift and tuck yourself into my hood."

Her sleepy eyes blinked up at me, then she yawned once and did as I asked, slipping into the cub-size version of my jungle cat form, a single strand of a collar around her neck allowing her to keep her clothing with her, the same way I could.

The same way all half-Jinn could.

That realization caught me off guard and I stared at her as she climbed into the hood on my cloak and dug her claws into the material to hold tightly. A thought for another time, when I wasn't busy trying to keep us all alive.

The screech of the massive birds came again, and I dared a look back. Torin and his son stood side by side, keeping the birds' attention on them as they reared up and struck at the enormous talons that came for them.

They were buying us time, but we weren't going to have a heck of a lot of that when the birds realized what was happening.

"You cannot beat me, even here, in the rabisu's body," Steve/Asag said. "Are you such a fool as to even try?"

I pulled Lilith from her scabbard on my back and felt that urge to kill rush up through me, then pulled my gun out in the other hand. "Better a witty fool, than a foolish wit."

Lila barked a laugh. "Bingo."

Steve/Asag snorted. "You will not survive your

trip through this domain without my blessing. A blessing I will not give. While I control the rabisu, you will be hunted even through the morning. I care not for their lives."

I stared at him, my heart pounding because I strangely thought of Steve as a friend. "Steve is stronger than you think." I had no such idea if he was, but I needed Steve to fight for his people, and in turn, that would mean he was saving us. *Come on, Steve. Don't be a Steve*, I thought, *be something better*.

He glared at me and bared his fangs, following it up with a loud ass snarl. "You will die now." His face fell and his eyes cleared for a split second, and Steve came through loud and clear. "Be not afraid of greatness. Some are born great, some achieve greatness, and some have greatness thrust upon them. You, I think, are the last of those. Kill me if you must. I will do all I can to keep my children at bay. Promise me you will see this through. That you will end Asag and free my children."

Damn it, another promise I could not turn away from. "I promise."

His eyes flicked back to the orange, and he shook his head. "What did he say to you?"

"He said I am as wise as I am beautiful," I whispered, "and that I'm to kick your ass into the beyond."

Steve/Asag snarled but took a step back and that was the answer I needed. He wasn't sure if he could take me.

There was no sound of chirping and the few rabisu I could see seemed to be . . . in some sort of limbo? Whatever hold Asag had on Steve, the master rabisu seemed to be holding his children still. I waved at the unicorns that bunched around me. "Go, the way is clear, get to Mamitu's holding." Goddess, I hoped I was right about that.

The unicorn herd took off at a full gallop, leaping into the jungle, trusting my word.

Steve/Asag stared hard at me. "I am trying to hold him back."

That was Steve, and then he shook his head, fighting himself.

I pulled Reyhan out of my hood and set her in the cave, and quickly strung up the cloak. "Lila, in here. If I die, you can fly them across one at a time."

Lila shot me a glare. "You better not die, or I'll kick your ass myself."

I turned to face Steve/Asag, smiling at her words. "I don't plan to die today, or anytime soon."

Lila sat in front of the cave.

Steve/Asag took another step back and it was obvious Asag had fully taken control. His orange eyes glowed bright as he whispered a single word. "Kneel."

I felt nothing, no buzzing in my skull, no moment of weakness, but my knees buckled, and I went to the ground as if my strings had been pulled. There was no passage of time that I saw and yet he was no longer so far away from me, but crouched in front of me, his hand on my jaw.

"You are a fool to think you are strong enough to stay the song of a rabisu from taking control of you."

Lila was screaming at me, Reyhan called to me, both in their own ways, but those sounds were like a buzzing in my ears, there, but not, nothing but white noise. I stared into his eyes. "I killed my ex-husband, you know that?"

His eyebrows raised as his hand tightened on my jaw and he tipped my head sideways, prepping me for a strike. Would his bite be what it took to take hold of me and control me? Or would he just take my life and be done with it?

My hand gripped the sword and I let the barriers down that I kept in place. Steve had known I carried Lilith.

Asag did not.

Her words fill my mind instead of the call of the rabisu, the blood lust rising in a wave that terrified me, touching on every animalistic instinct

I had. But if I didn't let her help me, I was going to die right then and there. Her words, her power began to drive out whatever hold he had over me.

The barriers I'd set up to keep her from taking control dropped one by one, and I let her into my soul.

*Kill him, strike him down, bleed him dry.*

I twisted my wrist and thrust the sword upward, but Steve danced backward, the blade just missing him as I stood.

His eyes locked onto the sword. "Impossible. Mamitu hid her!"

"And I felt her call to me," I growled as I rolled the handle in my palm. "I held her sister the flail long enough to know a powerful weapon when I see one."

His eyes locked on me. "No matter, you will die this night, and I will bury your bones in a bog."

We circled around one another and the night erupted with chirping all through the trees, above the rocks, behind us, cutting off any escape.

"I doubt that," I said. "Where there is life, there is hope."

He laughed at me. "Where there is hope, there is also despair. You are a fool to believe that this world will bow to you, that you will always win. You are a fool to believe that you will not lose anyone in the travels you take, in the journey your feet find you walking. I am Asag, the first of the Gallu demons, and I *own this world*."

His words stabbed at me and at a fear that haunted my sleep. "There are always losses."

"But are you willing to give the ones you love a clean death? Are you willing to give them a way to free themselves from the madness you bring? You are going to bring all the chaos down on this world, and while that is what it will take for change, do not think for one second that you will see it through unscathed."

His words were . . . haunting because he was not wrong and I knew it. "I know that. I've known that with every battle I've walked into, every battle that I've been thrown into. But I will not let you take my mind, and I will not let you kill my friends. I'd rather give in to her." I lifted my sword and her cooing words filled my blood with rage and the desire to taste his death.

I took a half step toward him, swung the sword, pivoted as I changed the direction of the weapon and swept toward his legs instead.

He leapt up and at me, tackling me to the ground. I rolled hard to the side, driving him below me even as he whispered my name and that I was safe with him. My arms went soft as I put one hand to his throat.

And for a moment, I saw him as he had been.

The dark golden hair and the blue-green eyes, the smile that lit up the sun, the slightly pointed ears, the beauty of the face that made my heart break for thinking I could or would dare to mar it.

My fingers on my sword hand started to ease from the handle.

*He will kill those you love. Kill him first.*

My grip tightened and I whipped the blade forward, the point resting at the hollow of his throat. Steve stared up at me, no longer the beauty he had been, but the rabisu once more.

Asag had fled.

"My people will die. You are right about that. Trapped as monsters and dying as such." His eyes closed. "Make it swift then."

The blade whispered of revenge, of safety, and of all the things that I had learned in the past. That people lied and cheated, that they were not what they said they were, that they broke promises and they hurt those they said they loved. That I should finish this as it was and not trust another soul.

I pressed the tip of the blade harder into his neck, and he did not fight me.

"Asag is gone." I spit the words out as sweat dripped down my face. Not from the fight with him, but from holding the sword back. Like it had a life of its own, it itched to drive the rest of the way into Steve's throat.

"He fled for fear my death would take him too," Steve said. "Quickly now, before he is back."

Jaw ticking, I pulled the blade away from his neck.

"This world needs to be better," I said. "Let us pass, Steve. I do not want to kill you. Hope is something that should not always run with despair."

A shriek of the giant birds made my skin crawl. Two fights going on at once. I could only pray that Torin and his son had fared as well as I and still had their skin intact as they held the birds back on the open plains, buying time for the rest of the herd to flee.

I stood and took a step away from Steve, just in case Asag popped back in. Steve lay on the ground a moment longer. "You fought off her call."

"I have experience fighting off the urges to use a weapon bent on destroying who I am," I said softly. "This one is no different in many ways."

He touched his throat and the bead of blood that rose to his fingertips. "Do not be so sure of that. She is treacherous and is only testing your boundaries. You have not seen her full strength."

I didn't wait for him to stand. I went to the small cave and scooped up my cloak, the cub that was Reyhan and Castor. The pounding of hooves up the slope turned me in time to see Torin and his son crest the ridge behind us, the birds flying fast behind them.

Well, shit, looked like we weren't done yet at all.

I all but threw the others up on Torin's back. I leapt up and Lila landed on my shoulder.

"Go, I will hold my children as best I can," Steve said. "Kill those you must to pass."

I nodded and Torin leapt forward into the jungle as the massive birds swept in behind us. This was going to be a fun ride. I could just feel it.

## 24

I didn't have to urge our unicorn mount Torin to go. He took off and plunged into the jungle where the giant birds could not reach, plowing through the undergrowth. Branches and leaves slapped at my arms, legs, and face. Our three smaller companions hid under my cloak. Lila slid down into the hood, Reyhan sat in front of me and Castor sat behind me. Torin's son galloped along to my right, blood running down his left shoulder in a trio of talon gashes.

"That blood is going to draw the rabisu," I said. "Go as fast as you can."

We followed the pathways made by the rest of the herd, and that helped us with the speed of things, but not by much.

Silence rode us as we galloped through the

midnight-dark jungle with not a single sound around us of chirping. At least not right away.

Torin kept up a steady pace, leaping logs, sloshing through creek beds, working his way around every obstacle laid out in front of us with a speed and precision that would have made Balder envious. His son stumbled more than once but kept up.

By my guess we were halfway through the jungle when it happened.

The chirping started as a single call that I wanted to believe I was only hearing out of stress and the strain of listening for their calls.

"That was one," Lila said from my hood. "I don't know if we are even halfway through the jungle."

"We don't stop until we are on the other side. No matter what happens, we go hard. We need to get the herd and Reyhan to Mamitu's." I wanted to go straight to Maks, but it looked like that wouldn't be the case now. First things first and all that jazz.

The Vessel of Vahab was still in its sack, tied to Torin's mane. I touched it. We were almost there. We were almost back. I'd drop the damn thing off and head straight south for Maks.

Another chirp sounded louder and closer than the first and my anxiety spiked. Not because I couldn't kill them, but because there were so many to protect this time.

"Torin, we have to keep them from the rest of the herd," I said softly, knowing he'd hear me. I leaned forward as a blur of movement raced for a moment beside us—eyeless, slits for noses—the image there and gone in a flash. We had no more of the herbal powders that would allow for us to draw the wounds clean.

I looked to his son. "You need to go faster, get well ahead of us." I transferred Reyhan and Castor to his back. Her big eyes stared up at me. "He will take you to Mamitu. Torin, we need to fall back, go slower, let the rabisu come to us."

He bobbed his head, his horn flashing. Lila clenched my shoulder. "This is a terrible idea, even if it's right."

A screech above us said it all. The big fucking birds hadn't given up either. Why I thought Mamitu would protect the unicorns I didn't know. What I did know was that on flat ground they would have their best chance.

I tugged on Torin's mane and he slowed his pace until he was walking. Walking through the jungle of the rabisu.

"Ready, Lila?" I smiled at her. "Wanna sing with me? Nothing but the best, of course."

She stared at me like I'd lost my mind. Until I

started to sing, using a tune from my childhood. I belted the words out, loud as I could with no care for carrying a good tune, only wanting the words to carry through the jungle and pull the rabisu back to us.

"O Mistress mine where are you roaming?

O stay and hear, your true love's coming,

That can sing both high and low."

I took a breath and looked at Lila with my eyebrows raised. She shook her head but she did join in on the rest of the song, our combined voices making quite the racket. Torin even helped out with a whinny here and there.

"Trip no further pretty sweeting.

Journeys end in lovers' meeting,

Every wise man's son doth know.

What is love, 'tis not hereafter,

Present mirth, hath present laughter:

What's to come, is still unsure.

In delay there lies no plenty,

Then come kiss me sweet and twenty:

Youth's a stuff will not endure."

We trailed off—off key no less—and a series of chirps that rolled like a wave blew up all around us. "I think we have their attention now," I said. "You think they like Shakespeare?"

A flurry of movement came at us from my

sword side and I swung Lilith, taking two heads at once. "Time to go!" Lila yelped.

The stallion grunted and took off once more, leaping over a trio of downed logs, his hooves pounding into the ground, going from a walk to a full speed gallop in that one leap.

The calls of the rabisu, and flashes of their pale skin through the darkness and the jungle foliage came from all directions, including in front of us, which was to be expected if rather unwelcome. Torin gored several, tossing them out of his way, their blood spraying through the air and splattering the three of us.

He was doing all he could, and I knew there was a chance we might not make it out alive. I knew it.

"MY CHILDREN, let them pass!" Steve's voice boomed through the air and the rabisu gave a pause, listening to him.

*Please, let his control hold* was my only thought.

Torin turned on even greater speed and I knew we were getting close to the other side of the jungle. But would Steve's call to his children keep them off us long enough? I leaned over Torin's neck, hugging close to him, Lila pinned between us.

"I don't hear them," she said. "He did it. For once, Steve came through and—"

The chirping whipped up around us, answering us far too clearly. They would not listen even to their creator with a bounty set at their table.

"A trap, they will set up another trap. That's what I would do if I were trying to stop intruders permanently," I said, doing what I could to see if there were any more in front of us. "Lila, go up, see if you can spot what's happening ahead. If they are going to try to barricade us in, maybe we can avoid it."

She launched out from inside between me and Torin, shooting up through the trees before any spindly long fingers could take hold of her.

The chirping intensified and from above Lila shouted, "They are ahead of us, but the line isn't solid yet. The other unicorns got through, I think! This would be the time to tell that stallion to use his super speed if he's got any left."

Except that I knew that his super speed had been on open ground. Not in the middle of a fucking jungle where he was having to dodge and leap, slowing him down.

Sweat slicked his coat for the first time and I had no doubt that we were nearing the end of his energy.

I pulled the shotgun out and filled it with ammo, then lifted it to my shoulder, sighting to the right of Torin's head. "Don't move, my friend."

The first pale glimmer of rabisu skin between the foliage ahead of us was all I needed. I squeezed the trigger and sent one of the grenades flying toward it.

For just a moment, I thought the grenade was a dud. Then the thing exploded, and the world was on fire, and the chirping turned to screams as the rabisu burst into flames. A hand grappled at my leg and I kicked it off, swinging down with the butt of my gun, knocking the rabisu free.

Those same fingers shot in from both sides and behind us. I'd cleared the path in front if we could just get to it.

They raked down Torin's white hide, scoring him deeply even as I did all I could to fight them off. His footsteps slowed, not enough maybe for the rabisu to realize but I could feel the shift in his body, the slight hesitation as he fought to get through the jungle.

Rabisu hung from his tail and I swung around, pointed the shotgun and squeezed the trigger, blowing the heads off two. Well, partially anyway; enough that their hands went limp and the drag on his body eased.

"Almost there!" Lila yelled. "A hundred yards and you're clear!"

Torin blew out a sharp bugling call and the rabisu chirped like mad as they swarmed toward us still, more and more coming. Ants, Jasten had said they were like ants, and he was not kidding.

Ahead was a glimmer of open night sky, a tantalizing moment that I lost as hands snatched me and yanked me off Torin's back. He slowed and turned as I fell, his magic that held me on broken by the sheer force of numbers.

"Go, go!" I yelled at him as I fell to the ground of the jungle, letting my body step between doorways, taking on the shape of my house cat form. The change in size meant the rabisu lost their grip on me. I stumbled forward, caught my bearings and ran for the south end, trailing a bolting Torin. From where I was, I could see how many claw strikes he'd gained.

I dodged and ducked, dived and rolled between rabisu legs and hands, using my size once more to my advantage. There was a moment when I thought the jungle would never end, and then we were out in the open air, the rabisu screeching to a halt behind us, held back by some force we could not see.

That alone should have worried me more.

I raced across the open flat land toward a heaving, struggling to breathe Torin. I could get out the last of the herbs, we could slather it all over him and then we could get him to Mamitu. She would help. She had to.

He reared up suddenly, the moonlight catching the sheen of his coat and the glimmer of his horn, and then the sky went dark. A whoosh of wings and his body was enveloped by a set of talons that made him disappear except for his head.

I shifted to two legs and pulled my shotgun from my back. "Over my dead body, mother cluckers!" I had two grenades left. I launched one and hit the massive bird in the side. It screamed, stumbled in the air, and then slammed into the ground, Torin still clutched in its claws.

My own legs were numbing with the claw strikes of the rabisu and I had to fight to keep them going, to get to him. I knelt at his side and pulled Lilith from my back, and easily cut through the dying bird's talons.

"Hang on, we'll get you to Mamitu," I said, already feeling the effects of my wounds, the venom creeping through my body, not just my legs. Shit, shit, shit!

Torin whinnied softly and pushed his muzzle into my hand.

*My time is done. Take it for my son. Stop the demon.*

## 25

T he wind ruffled the feathers of the dead giant bird, the only sound as the chirping of the rabisu from the jungle faded behind us.

I blinked through a sudden rush of tears as Torin's horn fell from his head to the ground.

"No," I whispered. "This cannot be. You have to fight!"

He nuzzled me again and closed his eyes, his breath slowing on my fingers, then stopping.

Stopping. My heart clenched and I fell forward onto his neck, barely able to get the words out, but needing desperately to say them. "No. This isn't how it's supposed to end."

I stroked his face to the spot where his horn had shed. The spot was smooth as if it had been a wound for many years. I found the horn and wrapped my hand around it, tugging it close to my chest. I didn't know how I was going to get this to his son, who'd run off toward Mamitu when I was myself closing in on death. Where was Lila? That thought was slow to grow in my skull as I pitched forward, laying my head on Torin's neck, breathing in the smell of the plains and a spring wind.

The fog rolled over me once more and I stood in that line between light and dark for a second time. The darkness to my left filled with laughter. "She's dying again. Is this normal? Shouldn't she be unbeatable if she is a hero the world needs?"

From my right was the brightness and the white light that was beyond pure. The same woman stepped forward and stared at me. I shrugged. I mean . . . what could I say?

"The unicorn gave his life to carry you through this first challenge. He saw something in you worth dying for." She held up her hand, and a spray of sparkles flowed off her. "Those around you will die, little cat. They will die because you bring chaos in order to bring change. If you die now, there will be no change."

I stared at her. "Who are you?"

She smiled. "I am a demon."

I turned to look into the darkness. "You, too, I suppose?"

That one stepped forward and nodded, his skin as brilliantly red as before, his grin menacing. "You would suppose right. This is the land of demons, and we are the keepers of the realm. Because you are here, we have the final say in your moment of death."

I swallowed hard. "You let Torin die then?"

"He chose his moment of death. It was that or be owned by the Storm Queen," the woman said softly. "He is no creature to allow captivity or to give her his power." She tipped her head to my hand where I still gripped his horn. "But he trusts you with his power."

I stared at her and she smiled. "We cannot take your soul while you hold the horn. Torin gave it to you so you would survive."

My heart crumpled along with my legs as I went to the ground. "He would have survived if he'd kept it?"

"Yes," they said in unison. "Your heart is the key."

I opened my eyes, found myself staring at the bleeding underbelly of the big bird, its blood staining Torin's hide. I pulled the horn toward my body, turned it and pressed the tip against my breastbone, just above my heart.

The horn flared and heat ripped through me as the sun rose in the east, flooding the land with the warmth of the desert morning. Memories that were not my own cascaded through me.

Like a conversation witnessed from long ago.

A young, spindly-legged black colt danced at his father's side as they trotted through the desert.

*You will find the one who will bring peace to our land. But you must give up your horn.*

Torin looked down at the colt and nuzzled him with a gentle touch that could only be a father's love. But it was the tear that slid down from his dark eyes that caught at me. *There can be no other way. I see no other path. It will be treacherous. There will be those who hurt you before you find her. But find her, you must, and protect her with everything you are to bring her here.*

The colt looked up at his father, and dipped his head, his tiny horn barely a nub sticking out of his forehead. *She will be my friend?*

Torin lifted his head and he looked in my direction as if he could see me then, a crossing of two times in this single memory. *She will love you as if you are a part of her family, and she will bring you home to us. You are the greatest sacrifice I could give to see the demon abolished, my son. I would not send you if there was any other way.*

The colt bobbed and danced. *It is an adventure, and I will find her. I will bring her home.* He bowed his head and his horn fell off at his father's hooves. That tiny nub gone.

A muzzle pressed into the back of my neck, whiskery lips moving across my skin and then a long lick of a tongue. I opened my eyes and reached back with my free hand, not entirely sure if I was awake, dreaming, maybe even dead. Who the hell knew?

Rolling carefully, I looked up into the face of my boy. Balder stared down at me, then his eyes went past me to Torin, silent and still in death.

He snorted and leaned in and touched his father's neck, flared his nostrils and then gave a low whinny, his head drooping.

"I'm sorry," I whispered. "I . . ." He stuffed his head against my chest, and I grabbed hold of him in a hug as a tear slid down his cheek. I didn't know how Balder was here, and with much of his magic gone, and my own, there was no way to converse as we had before. I leaned once more to Torin and untied the Vessel of Vahab from his mane.

Balder lifted me to my feet and I held out the horn. "He wanted you to have this."

My horse that was not a horse shook his head, then reached around and touched the saddlebags still attached to him. I went to his side and tucked the horn and the Vessel of Vahab inside, then put the shotgun in its sheath that sat under my right leg, and only then did I notice the second horse. Black as the night, but the horse was no Batman.

"Who is this?" I held a hand out to her and she sniffed then licked, looking for a treat. I took hold of her reins and saw she wore Batman's tack. My heart picked up speed as I saw Maks's bedroll tied to the back.

"Balder, what happened?" I found my way to his side and mounted, still holding her reins. He danced under me and I urged him forward. "We'll figure this out."

I paused for one last look at Torin, except that he was gone, with nothing but a bloom of brilliant white flowers growing where his body had been. I blew him a kiss. "Thank you, my friend. I will never forget you."

I had no idea where Lila was, but I had a suspicion that was confirmed as we galloped up the hill that led out of the valley to the open strip that would take us to Mamitu's. She flew near the head of another unicorn, bringing back help.

She shot to me, and hit me in the chest, nearly taking me out of the saddle. "I was bringing help! Reyhan and Castor are with the others, headed for Mamitu!"

I wrapped her tight in my arm. "Help found me. Balder found me."

He snorted and bobbed his head up and down. The unicorn approaching us fell in beside us, big eyes sneaking looks at Balder and the mare. "We have to hurry," I said and leaned into Balder.

He leapt forward, so like his father my heart cried out. I clamped down on the grief and pain, pushing them aside for now. Balder took off, the unicorn on our left keeping pace without an issue. I was worried that the mare on our right would struggle, but within a few strides I realized we were holding her back.

She was like Balder, a hornless unicorn.

I leaned over his neck, Lila hanging tightly to me as we raced toward Mamitu's castle. If I could have thrown the Vessel of Vahab at her right then, I would have done so and continued south to find Maks.

Lila tapped my chest. "Torin?"

I shook my head. "No. The big bird . . . the rabisu . . . I couldn't save him." The whispered confession's pain cut through me. I couldn't save him. Please, goddess of the desert, let these not be the words I have to say about anyone else.

Balder set a blistering pace and we crossed the chunk of desert and approached the rock quarry that would lead us to Mamitu's castle.

Hours felt like days in the mad race to put

distance between us and the jungle, the birds, everything. All so we could get to Maks.

There was a flurry of red-robed ghouls as we approached, waving and cheering us on. I didn't care.

Balder charged through the weaving tunnels of rocks and took us all the way to Mamitu's castle where the door stood wide open. I clung hard to Balder, feeling the weakness finally hit me.

Maybe because I thought we were safe.

Balder slid to a stop sending up a spray of grass at Mamitu who sat on her wooden bench, flowers and chunks of dirt all around her. I dismounted and pulled out the Vessel of Vahab from my saddlebags.

I threw it at her feet where it clanged unceremoniously.

She stared at it for a second. "You did it."

"Do I detect a note of disbelief in your voice?" Lila snapped. "She said she'd get it, and she did. And we lost a friend along the way."

Only then did I look around the garden and take note of the unicorns tucked in amongst the trees and bushes. A few had scratches but on a quick count they were all there. The only one lost had been Torin.

"We made it!" Reyhan's voice cut through the sudden silence and she hopped off her mount and ran toward me, Castor held tightly in her arms like a limp doll. I scooped her up into a hug. "I knew we'd would make it. I told Mamitu that you were almost here."

Mamitu did not move from her seat. "Indeed, the child did tell me you would soon be arriving."

I didn't set Reyhan down. "Her father, Jasten, did he come to you here?"

"No." Mamitu shook her head. "His path took him to your mate, and they have been . . . taken."

Everything in me wanted to run, wanted to take after Maks.

But I was not a foolish teenager to think I could run and never drop, that I could be wounded and never bleed.

"We would stay the night, then leave in the morning for the south," I said.

Mamitu gave me the slightest of nods. "You have my permission to cross the mountains at any juncture you wish."

The Vessel of Vahab gave a sudden shake. "Tell me you bumped it," I said softly. "I cannot handle another monster, fight, run for my life, argue with a desert-damned fucking beast as to why I have every right to live!"

Yeah, I might have been yelling by the end of that bit of a rant. What can I say? It had been a rough week or two.

Mamitu shook her head. "The vessel is designed to hold Vahab until he is called forth. Now that he has been taken from his hidden spot, he will try to break free. If the Jinn I asked your mate to bring here had come, I could have handed him over to them. As it is, you must take the vessel with you."

I stared at her. "No."

She spread her hands to either side of her body. "And you must take the child. She cannot remain here. Her path lies with you."

My jaw ticked and I had no words for the anger that burned from me. "Want me to take all your ghouls while I'm at it? Make it a flouncing goddess-damned circus?"

Her eyes blinked up at me. "This is your path, Zamira of the western desert. Not mine. You must take all you bring with you, as each has its place in your journey, even if you don't know what that place is."

Lila shot forward to hover in front of her face. "And now you won't tell her, right?"

Mamitu bowed her head. "You have taken the first challenge by storm. Asag is wroth with me. He will arrive in three days' time to punish me. You must be gone by then. The first part of his punishment was to take my ability to see the future. The last thing I saw was his arrival."

If anything could have set me back on my heels, that was it. "Then I could stay. I could fight—"

She shook her head. "The time draws close, but this is not it. You must gain your powers back, Zamira. You must find your mate. Lila must find her heart. The steps are all there, and they must be taken for the dance to be complete."

Lila snorted. "I hate dancing."

## 26

I stood in Mamitu's castle garden, Lila and Reyhan beside me, and stared at the Vessel of Vahab lying in the grass. What I didn't expect was for Insha to shoot in and pull the fucking cap off.

"Let him rule! Let us be free of Mamitu and her slavery! Better to serve a man who has sense in his head than a woman ruled by her traitorous heart!" the little ghoul screeched. The liquid smoke that poured out of the vessel boomed with a roar that sent the unicorns hiding.

Mamitu cried out, "You fool! There is none who can contain him! There are no Jinn here!"

I threw Reyhan, still holding Castor, onto Balder's back. "Hide!"

And then I pulled Lilith from my back. Her

power raged into me, and there was nothing but death. Nothing but the desire to kill and maim and destroy. Which in this case was probably for the best.

The ghouls who got in my way lost their heads as I strode toward the still-throbbing vessel, more and more of the smoke pouring out, filling the green space, and darkening the sky with an unnatural light.

Lila was screaming and I pointed at her. "Stay back!" I didn't know if it was because of the vessel or Lilith. Both were a danger to her.

I fought to keep myself in some kind of check, but I couldn't stop my blade from cutting down any who were in my path.

The blade had hold of all my anger, all my wrath, and I fought hard to contain it. To slow its need to kill.

The smoke began to clear, and a figure stood in front of me. Dark hair hung from his head in hundreds of tiny braids, and his skin reminded me of a bronzed statue I'd seen once. He tipped his head to the side and stared at me with eyes of clearest green, not so different from my own.

"You hold a weapon I created. You think it would strike me down?" He smiled, brilliant white teeth flashing, and his power crept out around us. I could still see through him as though he wasn't quite all there yet.

"I've heard that line before," I said. "But it is not the weapon I think you should fear."

He still smiled at me. "Only a Jinn could put me back now, only a Jinn could rule me."

His words were all I needed. That and little belief in myself. I forced my palm open and Lilith dropped to the ground. "Then you will serve me."

His eyebrows went up as I bent and picked up the vessel. The metal was cold like the snowy peaks of the Ice Witch. I held it tightly. "You are not free."

"I was the one who freed him. He is mine to command!" Insha shrieked from my side, scrabbling for the vessel.

Lila dropped from the sky right onto his head and yanked him backward. They tumbled to the ground. "Hurry, Zam, do whatever you are going to do!"

I held the vessel and looked at Vahab, looked at the forest that was shrinking and Mamitu's body that was right before my eyes slumping, the life sucked out of her as Vahab stood stronger with each second.

Drawing on every ounce of alpha I had in me, I said one word. "Stop!"

Vahab stared at me. "You cannot control me."

Now, in another time, another place, I might have agreed. But I was tired, bruised, heartsick, and I knew I had a damn long journey ahead of me. "Get in the vessel now before you make me do something we will both regret."

He stared at me, leaned forward and put his face close to mine. Inspecting me. "Who are you?"

"NOW!" I barked the word and he jumped back. And then shook his head like he couldn't believe he'd done even that.

I held the vessel out. "Get. In. Asag is coming. You think he's going to let a power like you just float about all willy-nilly? He'll take control of you and make you his pet. At best."

That gave him pause and I shook the vessel at him. "Get in. And we will discuss the parameters of your release."

He grimaced and his muscles trembled even as he took a step toward the vessel. Fighting my call, but still doing as I commanded. "How are you strong enough to compel me?"

I raised my chin and my eyebrows at the same time. "Because I am a fucking queen of the desert, and alpha in every way that matters, and I'm about done with the horseshit of idiots who think they can rule because of strength instead of heart."

I snapped my fingers and he slid back into the

vessel, grumbling all the way like nothing more than a reluctant teenager.

As soon as the smoke was in, I grabbed the lid and snapped it shut on him. I looked at Mamitu who sat still slumped in her chair, her hand to her chest. "Now. What was that about Asag?"

\* \* \*

LESS THAN AN HOUR LATER, RESUPPLIED AND WITH Mamitu's warning ringing in my ears that Asag was very much on his way, and that I wasn't ready yet to face him, I did the only thing I could.

I set Castor on the back of Balder's brother, now the lead stallion of the herd, and sent them west toward the Stockyards and my own brother, Bryce. The Bright Lion Pride would take the unicorns in and protect them, and Castor would be that much closer to the land of Dragon's Ground.

I looked at Lila sitting on my shoulder as we watched the herd leave. "You sure you want him to go? He's not much to take with us."

She bobbed her head once. "He's a good one, but he's not for me. And he's safer to go on with them." She flicked her wings. "And I asked him to come, but he said he didn't much like adventure."

"Definitely not for you then."

Reyhan sat on the back of the black mare she'd dubbed Dancer. She looked awfully small on the tall horse. "I like her," the girl said. "Is she mine?"

I smiled. "For now."

From my back, the blade of Lilith hummed softly and I closed my eyes, hearing the whispers of death and battle just under the surface. Dropping her in Mamitu's garden had been one of the hardest things I'd ever done, and still, I itched to pull her from my back and kill something.

I turned Balder to the south. "Storm Queen, huh?"

Lila snorted. "Like she's something fancy pants, right?"

I nodded, but my thoughts had turned inward. What was I willing to risk to save Maks? I already knew the answer, but I wondered if I would fully understand the cost. I wondered if he would understand just how far I would go to bring him back. Maybe he did. I'd saved him from madness before.

But this felt . . . different. A woman's hold on a man she felt was her own could be a deadly thing. This Storm Queen, if she truly meant to take Maks to her bed to produce an heir, wasn't just hurting him. She was hurting me. She was hurting our relationship.

It felt wrong on so many levels. I dropped my hand to the Vessel of Vahab and considered the options.

Vahab knocked from inside the vessel. "You said we'd talk."

"Not right now." I smacked it hard and he yelped. "When we stop for the night, then we will talk."

By then maybe we'd have enough distance between us and Asag.

By then, I'd need to come up with a plan to save Maks, the hatchlings, and kill a demon bent on enslaving the entire desert.

Yeah . . . it was going to be a long day, and an even longer night.

aks lay strapped to the bed, with nothing more than a sheet over his waist. There were only a few candles lit around the room, but it didn't matter. His night vision was good enough to see the Storm Queen as she strode into the room, her robe flaring around her legs and giving him a rather clear view of the fact that she wore nothing beneath it.

His father whispered in his ear. "Zam is going to be pissed if you bed her."

He turned his head to the side to see Marsum, eyebrows to his hairline. Maks grimaced. "You have something helpful to suggest?"

"No, thought I'd just point out the obvious," Marsum said and then disappeared.

Maks rolled his head back to center and stared

up at the ceiling. Strapped down for the last half-hour, he'd been working hard at the bonds that held him which had only tightened the knots and made his fingers numb.

"Cute, did you think you would actually escape me?" She made her way to the side of the bed. "Did you try shifting?"

He schooled his face to give away nothing. Because, yes, he had tried shifting to no avail. He'd tried anything and everything to get out of the damn bed.

She laughed softly and trailed her fingers across his chest. "The last man I bedded had great power, but not such a fine body." Her hands dipped lower and he sucked in a sharp breath. "Fine indeed."

With a flick of her wrist, her robe knot untied and the entire thing slid to the floor. He stared at the ceiling, unable to fully believe this was happening as she climbed onto his body.

"You should relax and enjoy this. Just think of me as your mate. I doubt I'll catch with a single time having you inside me. I expect you will be in my bed for weeks."

His gorge rose and he turned his head to the side as his body heaved. She was not Zam, and there was no pretending otherwise.

Her slap across his face made stars burst in his vision.

Maybe that was why he thought he was seeing things as her massive guard stood in the doorway to her bedroom. "Lady, the rhuk are back. They bring one of their own."

The Storm Queen sighed and slid off his body. "Send him to the dungeon. Naked. No food or water."

His bonds were cut and he was heaved over the guard's shoulder, bare ass to the wind but he didn't care. He wasn't in her bed, and that was all that mattered for the moment.

The guard carried him behind the Storm Queen and they stopped as they went out onto the top parapet of the castle. The one carrying him turned so he was looking back at the scene as they headed across the rooftop to a far doorway. One of the massive birds lowered another, obviously dead, wings limp to the feet of the Storm Queen. She let out a cry and went to her knees, her fingers lightly touching feathers. "Who could do this? Who would dare do this?"

He stared at the big hole in the bird's side, seeing the shrapnel and the bits and pieces that told him exactly what had done it.

"A grenade," he said, then bit his own damn tongue. Fool, idiot! Why say anything? But he knew why, a very large part of him wanted this queen to fear touching him.

The Storm Queen turned to stare at him. She snapped her fingers and the guard dropped him to the ground. Hands still bound, he stared at her. "A grenade did that."

"Who would dare?" she snarled, and he let the smile slide over his face.

"My mate." He blinked up at her and a smile lifted his lips. "And she's going to hand you your ass on a platter."

**UP NEXT!**

Yes, there WILL be another Desert Cursed book!
In fact there will be two more! "Kingdom of
Storms" (Book 8) and "Realm of Demons" (Book 9)

. . .

But until then, how about I keep you busy reading
something else?
My first series "The Nevermore Series" is a love
story but of course, in my own twisted fashion ;)
Sundered
Or check out another series set in the World of the
Walls with
Venom and Vanilla

## ABOUT THE AUTHOR

Check out all my links to keep up to date, and my website for what's happening!
www.shannonmayer.com

CPSIA information can be obtained
at www.ICGtesting.com
Printed in the USA
LVHW020453290422
717484LV00011B/1322